A Place to Belong

A Study of Church Life in 1 Corinthians

Wendell Willis

JOURNEY BOOKS

An SPC Publication
Austin, Texas 78765

A complete Teacher's Manual with copy masters for student
EXPLORER'S SHEETS for use with this paperback is available
from your religious bookstore or the publisher.

Unless otherwise indicated, scripture quotations are from the
Revised Standard Version of the Bible, copyrighted in 1946,
1952, and 1971 by the Division of Christian Education,
National Council of Churches, and used by permission.

When noted, quotations are from the Holy Bible New International
Version © 1978, New York International Bible Society. Used
by permission of Zondervan Bible Publishers.

When noted, quotations are from The New English Bible, © 1961,
1970 by The Delegates of the Oxford University Press and
The Syndics of the Cambridge University Press. Reprinted
by permission.

When noted, excerpts are from The Jerusalem Bible,
copyright 1966 by Darton, Longman and Todd, Ltd. and
Doubleday and Company, Inc. Used by permission of
the publisher.

Edited by Paul Learned
Cover designed by Tom Williams

Printed in the U.S.A.
Library of Congress Catalog Card Number 82-80356
ISBN 0-8344-0119-3
2 3 4 5

Contents

3

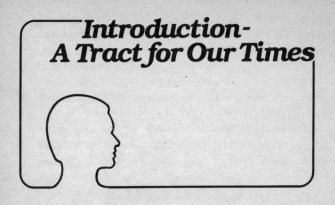

Introduction- A Tract for Our Times

The church in the twentieth century is strikingly similar to the Corinthian church of Paul's day. Like the Corinthians, our society is in rapid flux and is characterized by extreme mobility, shallow commitments, competing faiths, and, above all, great individualism. We today identify with their need to belong. In his first letter to the Corinthians Paul addresses these issues that threaten the church as a place to belong.

Sectarianism. The church at Corinth divided into disputant groups. Some aligned themselves behind Christian leaders (1 Cor. 1), although probably without the leaders' approval. This led to elitism, with some members boasting of their "maturity" and superior gifts before others. Even the Lord's Supper became an act of division instead of unity (11:17-34).

The Spirit. Paul has a deep appreciation for the work of the Spirit in Christian life, but he differs with the Corinthians on *how* the Spirit works. For the Corinthians, the Spirit was a means to escape the "slings and arrows" of daily life into a mystical world of special knowledge and wonders. Physical concerns (1 Cor. 5, 6) were overcome by possession of the eternal Spirit.

The church. The Corinthians had no conception of church life. For them, faith was a personal matter, and each believer sought his own spiritual well-being. Thus, the ethical actions of some with dangerous habits (1 Cor. 8) were personal concerns, not church issues. The Lord's Supper was reduced to several individual private meals (11:17-34).

The cross. The Corinthians believed that Jesus *delivers out of this world*, rather than *rules life within the world*, and this belief is the source of many Corinthian failures. For the Corinthians, Christ's lordship was swallowed up by his role as Savior to such a degree that even resurrection was unnecessary to those fully possessing the Spirit (1 Cor. 15).

Worship. The Corinthians experienced the life of the Spirit especially in worship. Through worship the heavenly life was manifested in spiritual gifts and angelic tongues. The Corinthians' worship was an escape from the meaningless world of earthly life, instead of a preparation for serving God in this life.

Then and Now

In many ways today we experience the same kinds of problems the Corinthians did. We too are tempted to form cliques and look down our pious noses at those whom we deem less Christian than ourselves. Believers who regard business practices of Monday unrelated to spiritual matters of Sunday cultivate an escapist faith. Worship that draws a thick line of distinction between what goes on within the church building and what takes place in the parking lot parallels the same fatal division of sacred and secular life that corrupted Corinth.

But of all the similarities, the two most pervasive and destructive are a misunderstanding of the church and a misconception of the cross.

5

Church members have obligations by virtue of sharing a common Lord and a common body. Although each of us comes to Christ as an individual, we do not live in him as individuals. In 1 Corinthians 12, we see that we all have great value to God. By working out our differences together toward a common goal, our life together in the body of Christ gives us a sense of belonging.

Finally, we need to relearn about the cross. The cross means that the pains and needs of others are more important than our own, that self-giving, not self-gain, is the mark of the Christian. These sentiments are certainly much easier to preach than to practice. Yet living for others is what makes the church *a place to belong*.

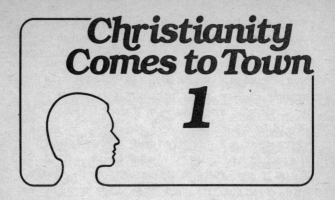

Christianity Comes to Town

1

1 Corinthians 1:1-9

Christians today are aliens in their own society. For years, this has been the case in some countries where only a small minority claim to be Christians. However, in recent years, many have come to have similar feelings about the United States as well.

Our fathers and forefathers lived in a culture that generally espoused Christian values, even among people who did not regard themselves as believers in Christ. The public institutions operated with prayers in Christ's name, schools had devotionals for children as part of the day's activities, and the slogan on the back of the currency, "In God We Trust," meant something. We do not need a Gallup poll to see how radically our national lifestyle has shifted in the last generation.

However, being a Christian minority in a pagan culture is not an experience new to this generation. Christians today are in a situation similar to the one faced by converts of the first century. This culture will not support and spread Christian values. Instead it regards both the Christian faith and Christians as out of step with the times.

Urban Threats

Christians today face many dangers that are perennial. Yet, in addition to these common sins and temptations, some new dangers face the church in the last years of the twentieth century. Three increasingly important pressures today relate to the rise of the secular city as the norm of American life.

First, there is a *widespread sense of rootlessness*. We are a mobile society. We travel a half-hour or more to our jobs or, in many cases, while we work. And we tend to move our families very often. The average family moves about every six years.

This high degree of mobility has severed the traditional strengths of location and family. The "castle" to which today's harried worker retreats each evening is regarded as a temporary dwelling, even if it is constructed of brick or stone. Similarly, our habit of moving has extremely narrowed the meaning of the word "family." Sociologists use the term "nuclear" family to describe the modern family, which commonly has only the most basic components: father, mother, and 1.3 children. The strength earlier generations drew from constant exposure to aunts and uncles, brothers and sisters, and even live-in grandparents is gone. Modern Americans have lost their connection to the past.

Second, this rootlessness results in a *sense of loss of personal identity*. My parents often described someone by saying: "You remember, he is John's nephew," or, "He's one of the Evans from east of town." A person's identity was rooted in his being a member of a long-standing family in the area. But in a highly mobile society, this means of identity is meaningless.

This loss of identity is illustrated in many ways. The disregard of bystanders during an assault is a sign of the modern inability to identify with others. We are "identified" by many numbers—driver's licenses, social security, telephone, business extension, credit card, and so on. Loss of identity is especially a problem in large cities where hundreds of thousands of highly transient residents gather. These modern city-dwellers remain lonely and afraid.

Third, one who has no sense of personal identity tends to *conform to others and their opinions*. In doing so, he finds his identity in others. This is why it is so hard for Christians to buck the pressure of the secular city. All—young and old—tend to conform under slight pressure.

In the late sixties I taught at a large state university. The youth rebellion was under way, and the hippie with long hair, ragged clothing, and obscene speech tried to express his rejection of his parents' conformist culture. Yet the students I saw daily looked as if they were following a manual on how to conform while nonconforming! Blue jeans, T-shirts, and sandals were their uniforms just as vested suits and button-down shirts were to my generation. All these pressures to conform seemingly threaten to inundate the church.

Urban Attractions

Although many of us may long for more secure days of rural life, we must realize that, in its beginning, Christianity spread in the cities. The reason is obvious. If Christians are to spread the gospel, they must go where men are—the cities. This is why Paul in Acts goes to Philippi, Ephesus, Athens, Thessalonica, Corinth, and other great cities.

In the first century, Corinth was a most modern city. It was strategic in commerce, culture, and military value, controlling the trade north-south in Greece and east-west from Rome to the eastern provinces.

In Paul's day Corinth had been recently resettled by

Caesar with Italian soldiers, freedmen from around the Empire, and Jews from Palestine. To this cross-cultural melting pot came the hucksters and the achievers, the philosophers and the priests. Many were attracted to a place to begin anew and make a fortune. The population was largely rootless. The city was based more on the gambler's dice than the farmer's hoe. Corinth's immoral reputation more than likely came from this transient, fortune-seeking population.

It is striking how much this picture of life almost 2,000 years ago parallels our own experience today. Although we have a greater balance between urban and rural population, America has many cities larger than ancient Corinth. Our large cities also house a rootless, estranged people, with a clash of values and cultures, lured there by various attractions. Today's television news programs take us to Houston, Los Angeles, and New York daily and in living color! Whether we like it or not, we are drawn to the beckoning, yet dangerous city.

Christianity Comes to the City

After Paul left Corinth, many problems arose as the young church tried to work out its salvation in a secular and pagan city. This book will look at some of the concrete issues that Paul confronted in Corinth. In one sense, Paul's answers are deeply embedded in the life of that city. This letter is very specific—a tract for the times.

Teachings that Christ posed in rural terms about sheep, seeds, and nets must now be obeyed in the midst of urban industry, commerce, crowds, and schedules. Our challenge, like that of the Corinthian church, is to follow Christ in a culture that is hostile to our faith.

The Church of God—in Corinth? (1:1-3)

Acts 18 gives the history of how Christianity came to be in Corinth. However, Paul begins his letter describing the same event from another perspective. First Corinthians 1:1-9 explains theologically that a church exists in secular Corinth because some responded to the preaching of the gospel. The Corinthian church's existence could be the result of the hard labor of Paul or the great need of the people, but Paul points to the cross as the decisive factor. Through the preaching of the word of the cross, men are drawn to the Crucified. The call of the gospel is the essence of the church—then and now.

When we stop to consider, it is really amazing that Paul could address a letter "To the church of God which is at Corinth." It seems as incongruous as a Jew writing to "the people of God in Samaria," or, in our day, "To the church of God on Bourbon Street." For Corinth was founded on sea commerce, and, like many other sea ports, it was not known for high moral standards.

To really appreciate what the gospel can accomplish, we need to know the nature of the Corinthians before they heard and believed the message of the cross. In 1 Corinthians 6:9-11 Paul gives a description of the members of the Corinthian church before they heard the gospel. After reading that passage we may stumble over Paul's address to those "called to be saints" in chapter 1, verse 2. Surely, we think, Paul wrote that with tongue pretty far in cheek. "Saints" indeed.

Yet, let's not be misled by the common usage of the word *saint* today. One most often hears the word in the expression, "He is a pretty good fellow, but he's no saint." Or in the apology, "Well, I'm no saint." These are moralizing uses that imply there are two levels of Christians—ordinary and extraordinary. Of course, the

11

Bible contains nothing of this distinction. If one is a Christian, then one is a saint.

The idea of calling is important in this letter, and Paul wastes no time addressing it. In 1:1-3, we see that this epistle is written by Paul, an apostle of Jesus Christ at *God's call* and by God's will. It is sent to the *church* in Corinth, which literally, means "the called out." This letter is by the *called* apostle to those in Corinth *called* to be saints.

The concept of those "called to the be saints" derives from the Old Testament picture of God's special relationship with Israel. In Exodus 19:6, God says to Israel, "You shall be to me a kingdom of priests, a holy (sainted) nation." This pledge follows God's calling of Israel from bondage. "Saints," then, refers not to the superiority of our lives, but to God's acceptance. It does not refer to moral perfection, but to God's call. That is why Paul never uses "saint" in the singular to denote some "super-Christian."

The claim that the word saint is not first of all a designation of those with moral superiority does not minimize the necessary connection of an ethical life and being saints. Those who are set apart as God's people ought to live lives that reflect the God they serve. Paul makes this connection many places, such as 1 Thessalonians 4:7, where he says God has called us to holiness of life (see also Eph. 4:1).

Equipped for Urban Survival (1:4-9)

All life, including Christian life, has three temporal aspects: its past, its present, and its future. All three are important to combat the three threatening pressures of the city: rootlessness, loss of identity, and conformity. To concentrate on one to the exclusion of the others will undermine our ability to survive in the city.

Past roots (1:4-6). In Corinth, as in cities today, the emphasis was upon the present. This was because the Corinthians had forgotten the original coming of faith and foresaw no needed improvement in the future. As a result, they became mistaken in many ways.

Many people today are drawn to the city seeking financial rewards. Wealth in coin, political power, and education are part of the lure of the secular city. The lure of riches is certainly nothing new; the Bible often speaks of being beguiled by this temptation. However, Paul says the Christian is rich in Christ (1:5). How is this to be understood in view of the many stinging things the Bible says about the dangers of wealth?

The difference is in the treasure. While the world counts riches in real estate and gold, Christians have their wealth in God's mercy (Eph. 2:4; Rom. 2:4) and glory (Rom. 9:23). Christ enriches those who call upon him (Rom. 10:12). And just as the gospel rejects the world's values in wisdom and power, it also dismisses its definition of wealth. What counts is the richness of mercy that we receive and show to others.

One of the richest men in Christ I have known never graduated from high school. He worked as a construction laborer. But he had a wealth of joy and friends and took pleasure in serving others. Many with great bank accounts will never have—or even understand—such a wealth as his.

By saying "which was given you," Paul reminds the Corinthians and us that whatever excellences we have in Christ are gifts from God (1:4). We ought to praise the Giver, not ourselves, nor even the gift. However, note what Paul does not say the Corinthians are rich in— faith, hope, and love.

One of the things of the past that Christians received from God's richness is the testimony of God confirmed among us (1:6). The Corinthians sought in various miraculous experiences to confirm their life in Christ. They thought personal experience of the Spirit was proof that they had full maturity in Christ even in the present.

Many Christians today seek some present proof of the reality and reliability of their faith. The recent charismatic revival in many churches is an example of this. Others seek proof in intellectual ways by acquiring great knowledge or constructing impressive theological systems. In this search, two things are overlooked—the confirmation of the gospel is in the past, and God, not men, confirmed it.

The word translated "confirm" comes from the legal vocabulary and refers to a substantiating witness or to the warranty to a deed of sale. The gospel is based on God's confirmation of Jesus (see Acts 17:31). The truth of the faith does not rest on the ability of preachers, the skill of thinkers, nor even the piety of believers. It is confirmed by the only one competent to declare it trustworthy—God himself.

Present identity (1:7). The present aspect to the Christian faith tells us who we are. In many Christians this is what is lacking. They remember with fondness the joy and meaning they had when first born into Christ. But as the years come and go, they have failed to find such fulfillment in their present Christian lives. Others live only in the future. Their faith is only a form of "fire insurance," which will be redeemable for value in the distant future. In the present, they struggle against life's needs on their own, never using the divine aid available now.

For those called, sanctified, and enriched by God, Paul points to two aspects of present Christian life—the fact that we are not lacking in spiritual gifts and the need to wait.

First, he tells the Christians in Corinth that they are not lacking in any spiritual gift. Interestingly, some in Corinth were sure others were lacking, and some believed they themselves were too. The Corinthians had developed a ranking for spiritual gifts—with speaking in tongues at the top—and declared that some Christians who lacked these gifts were second rate. Paul denies this. What the Corinthians lack is not gifts, but the wisdom to use them rightly.

Many Christians today may feel that they lack first class abilities or places of service. Some decide this by witnessing the members who are more prominent and visible and who seem to have better gifts. But what counts is not this gift or that, but the health of the whole body. Each gift, each member, is needed for the health of the whole.

A second aspect of Christian life in the present is waiting. There may be a no more accurate or frustrating description of disciples than "those who wait." Most of us have little patience for the need to wait. The modern city is, above all else, a place of the *now* with little hope for the future and few ties to the past.

The Corinthians had become so excited about their gifts and their wisdom and knowledge that they forgot about the future. They believed they had full possession of the Christian life now. As we will see, Paul uses some biting sarcasm in chapter 4 when he compares the overachieved Corinthians with the poor, failing apostles.

The Corinthians are not alone in wanting to have everything now. It is easy to find volunteers for church ministries that have an end to them. To work this week, to mow during the summer, even to teach for a year—all these obligations people are available to fill. But a task with no prospect of end, such as visiting nursing homes or doing janitorial work, is another matter. We have witnessed a succession of projects that many felt would convert the world in a few years. There were the cottage film strips, the area campaigns, the Exodus movements, the bus programs, and so on. All of these had their merit, but too many people had unrealistic expectations. They wanted some magic solution that would end waiting by full success.

But it isn't going to happen. Tension and waiting are part of the fabric of Christian living. The temptation of trying to settle everything is born from the desire not to wait, but to have. There are some things about the Christian life we cannot answer; we must leave them for the Lord's coming.

Future security (1:8-9). The need to wait leads us to consider the future for the Christian. We need not fear urban pressures to conform to evil. God has proved reliable in the past, he sustains us in the present, and he will continue to do so in the future. He will confirm us "guiltless" (better, "without reproach," NEB) on the Day of the Lord.

When we are told that we will be guiltless, we may flinch. We may think, "Perhaps some people, but not me." Many Christians have no confidence about judgment, and usually they are the most conscientious, dedicated people. They have come to despair because they do not realize that guiltless means acquitted, instead of "without flaw."

While you read the Corinthian letter, consider whether the church in Corinth would ever be morally faultless. A minister once remarked to me that he enjoyed studying Corinthians but was glad he didn't have to work with that congregation! No, guiltless does not mean without flaw. Because God has called us to be his people, sanctified us through the cross, no one can sustain charges against those he has confirmed as his people (Rom. 8:33-34).

16

That is the basis of a hopeful attitude toward the judgment.

Paul concludes his introduction to the letter with a reminder (1:9) that what gives security to our call as Christians is God himself. This is why Christians can be confident about the future, no matter how hostile their culture is to their faith.

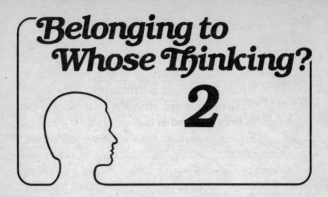

Belonging to Whose Thinking?

2

1 Corinthians 1:18–2:16

My wife and I have different views on dogs and cats. I prefer cats and she likes dogs. What I like about cats is that they are independent if not downright aloof. They will curry no man's favor. My wife, on the other hand, prefers dogs because they are always friendly and appreciative of any attention from their owners. Indeed dogs will beg to have the approval of their masters. When I think about it, what I prefer about cats are the traits my wife doesn't find attractive, and vice versa. We both agree most cats are characterized by aloofness and most dogs by friendliness, but we differ on the desirability of these attributes.

In a way, the gospel is like that. The same message from the same messenger at the same time is heard in radically different ways by various hearers. Some *hear*, and others only hear.

Misunderstanding the Cross

In 1 Corinthians 1 Paul notes how differently the gospel is perceived by different hearers. "For the word of the cross is folly to those who are perishing, but to us who are being saved it is the power of God" (1:18).

18

This statement follows a discussion of divisiveness (1:13-17), which Paul addresses with the message of the cross. Divisiveness results from a failure to understand the gospel. It is not the result of a disagreement over some minor secondary issues (Bible classes, benevolence, etc.). Divisive spirits arise when the word of the cross has not been believed in the church.

Paul preached the cross to the Christians in Corinth. Some accepted it, crediting their salvation to God alone and willingly taking up their daily crosses by serving others. Others, influenced by their humanistic, individualistic culture, misunderstood the cross. They credited their salvation to their own human efforts and wisdom. Further, they felt that God's calling them made them more spiritual and more important than others. They rejected the cross by demanding to be served rather than being willing to serve others.

The opposition between human wisdom and the word of the cross is not as simple as the curriculum we follow. The Bible, its history, and its interpretation is a legitimate area of academic study. Yet one can hear and know scripture exceedingly well and never have believed in the gospel. Remember it was not the unlearned and the irreligious who demanded Jesus' life from Pilate! Human pride rejects submission to and dependence on God.

A Foolish Message (1:18-25)

What is the problem with human wisdom, and what is the advantage of God's wisdom? How do we determine the one from the other? Why can't human wisdom accept the word of the cross? To answer these questions, let's look at some characteristics of human wisdom.

Human wisdom is self-centered. It begins with man and his abilities to think and know. This is the case with both the Gentile philosopher and the religious Jew. In both approaches—philosopher and religious master—God is placed on trial before human criteria. The roles are reversed and the creature tells the Creator what is acceptable. (See Rom. 1:18-32 for a description of pagan life as refusing to let God be God.) Jesus' cross is rejected by those who seek God by logic and those who base faith on miracles.

Human wisdom is disputatious and divisive. Divisiveness in the Corinthian church is what led into Paul's discussion of wisdom (1:10-17). The divisions had their origins in human wisdom, which is self-centered. Thus behind the party spirit and factional slogans is pride. There is safety in a party pride. Most of us are uncomfortable in boasting of our understanding and our achievements, but we can easily do that for our group. Shared pride seems somehow less blameworthy.

The same attitudes can be seen today. Scarcely is a new slogan used or a new argument published or a new speaker praised before men begin lining up pro or con. Arguments then are set forth and collected. Human wisdom, even among Christians, is always more argumentative than healing, more critical than serving.

Human wisdom is ineffective. Paul notes that, through its wisdom, the world did not find God. Indeed, the message of God confirmed mankind in his rebellion, for it became an occasion of stumbling. When Paul says that the gospel was an offense and an occasion for stumbling to Jews, he speaks from experience. He persecuted Christians for precisely that reason. It is likely that the argument he notes in Galatians 3:13, in which he quotes Deut. 21:23 to prove Jesus could not be the Christ, is one he believed before his conversion.

What makes human wisdom merely human is that it not only deals with practical matters instead of religious ones, but, more importantly, it neglects the cross. The "word of the cross" is the power of God to save (1:18) continually in our Christian lives as well as when we first believed. The cross is not only the means by which Jesus was executed. It is the symbol of all those who answer Jesus' summons to "take up your cross and follow me" and choose to serve rather than be served.

A Foolish People (1:26-28)

What sort of people put their faith in a message about a man who was killed on a cross? It is no accident that the church is seldom composed and less seldom led by the powerful of society. The powerful people—whether in office, finances, or education—usually stake their hopes in their own achievements. But the cross calls all human achievements into question. Paul uses this practical observation with the Corinthians (1:19). Look around at your members. Who is going to be impressed by most of you?

The choosing of the unlikely and the powerless is a parable of the message of the cross. What makes the gospel so hard to believe, on human grounds, is that it accepts the weak, the powerless, and the unexceptional. This is just the opposite of human wisdom, which favors the important, the powerful, and the "movers and shakers" of the world.

Celsus, an early critic of Christianity, inadvertantly confirms Paul's teaching when he says of Christians:

Their injunctions are like this. "Let no one educated, no one wise, no one sensible draw near. For these abilities are thought by us to be evils. But as for anyone ignorant, anyone stupid, anyone uneducated, anyone who is a child, let him come boldly." By the fact that they themselves admit that these people are worthy of their God, they show that they

21

want and are able to convince only the foolish, dishonourable and stupid.

The cross is a new event, but not a new approach, in God's manner of teaching his message to men. Consider the choice of Israel to be his people. If men had been in charge of selecting a nation to bear God's name and to be his witness in the time of Moses, human wisdom would have suggested Syria or Egypt, the two major powers of the day. But God chose a people that were slaves and fewer in number, stubborn in heart, precisely so that they could not boast of their achievements (Deut. 7:6-8). The pride of the wise and the powerful make them unlikely candidates for teaching God's message of service. Jesus himself is the prime example of the powerless proclaiming God's message (Phil. 2:6-10).

Let None Boast (1:29-31)

In this scathing attack upon the wise and powerful, there is a danger that Christians may think that only non-Christians are being rebuked. We must recall that the letter is written to the Christians in Corinth, not to the pagans. The effects of the world's standards seem to have been found in the church and had produced divisions. This was most obvious in the boasting that arose about various leaders. This boasting and pride are clear evidence that the cross had been exchanged for human wisdom.

God's motive for choosing the powerless is stated directly in 1:29, "So that no one may boast before him," (NIV). Notice that Paul does not say "So that no pagan," but that no one—pagan or Christian—may boast. Christians boasting of men (3:21) make clear that they have not understood the message of the cross.

Clearly the danger of boasting has not disappeared as the centuries have rolled on. Although the church today may claim it follows divine rather than human knowledge, the decisive test is the presence of boasting. When we point with pride to our achievements, or boast that we have done better than that congregation or that preacher, the message of the gospel is compromised.

A Foolish Preacher (2:1-4)

It is not uncommon for church members to claim that a sermon was not good or even not accurate. Rarely do we label a preacher "foolish." But in 1 Corinthians 1:18-28 Paul points out that not only are the words of the cross and the people who believe them out of step with human values—or "foolish"—but also those who deliver the words. In chapter 2 Paul shows how the wisdom of the world rejects the preacher of the cross as foolish.

By no means is Paul recommending preaching that is foolish because it is ignorant, crude, or ungrammatical. No one should take pride in having his message rejected and automatically assume this rejection confirms he has rightly presented the gospel. Still, Paul begins by reminding the Corinthians that his conduct among them was in full accord with a word about a cross (2:1).

Greek education was divided broadly into two avenues: rhetoric and philosophy. The proponents of these two approaches competed with each other for students, and both claimed their respective approach was the true path to excellence in life. In 2:1 *lofty words* and *wisdom* refer to these two schools of education. They are the *inward* (wisdom) and *outward* (lofty words) ways men sought to commend their beliefs to others to persuade them.

But Paul explicitly and intentionally rejects both approaches as incompatible with the message he preaches (2:2). Anyone who has read 1 Corinthians 13 is well aware that Paul could use great skill in persuasion. But in presenting the gospel he finds persuasion tactics inappropriate. Such tactics would empty the cross of its power (1:17). How so?

Many of us have heard public speakers, including preachers, who had great abilities to sway people. By using such techniques, the preacher may mistakenly present the gospel message in a way that denies its content—a cross. The cross shapes not only the *content* of Christian evangelism, but also its *style*. When one's faith depends upon the artful skill of a speaker or the impressive answers of a teacher, it is also at the mercy of a more skillful speaker or a more learned teacher. Any faith arising from human abilities is subject to other human abilities. The "believer" does not respond to the gospel; he responds to the speaker's cleverness. This is why Paul made the conscious decision not to rely upon customary means of persuasion.

The Message is God's (2:5)

Because there is a great possibility of misunderstanding, Paul restates the point of the contrast between human wisdom and God's foolishness. First Corinthians 2 is not a praise of silly talk or ignorance, nor does it laud offensiveness or buffoonery on the part of the speaker. The point is that human persuasion relies upon man's abilities, but the word of the cross is the power of God at work.

Most people view sermons solely as the art and skill of the man who speaks. It is true that men prepare sermons and deliver them. But since the gospel is God's message, its real power lies in him (1:18, 21, 24; 15:15). It is God who makes the appeal for reconciliation through the preacher's words (2 Cor. 5:20). This is because preaching is not merely humanwork, but the power of God (1 Thess. 1:4, 5).

An Advanced Wisdom? (2:6-15)

For centuries the monastic system claimed to offer a superior way for a few to attain a higher level of dedication than that achieved by the average person. Although we have rejected monasticism, some Christians still consider themselves superior to others, just as some did in Corinth.

A careful reader of 1 Corinthians 1 and 2 catches an apparent conflict beginning in 2:6. After all the talk praising God's foolishness and attacking human wisdom, it is somewhat of a shock to read that Paul does indeed know of a wisdom for the mature. Does Paul recognize two levels of believers—regular and honors?

In 1 Corinthians 2:7 Paul says that among the mature believers there is a secret and hidden wisdom. In the Greek this wisdom is referred to as a mystery. What Paul means by mystery here can easily be explained.

My father had a good friend who was a magician. Even if I tried to learn his tricks, he always refused to share the secrets. As a youngster I knew there was an explanation for what he did, but, because it was not explained to me, the tricks' mechanics remained a mystery. Similarly, the word *mystery* in the Bible does not mean something without explanation, but something that is not obvious to observers unless explained.

This is why the Christian wisdom is a mystery. Not because it is unexplainable, but because it is not obvious to those who encounter it. God's wisdom is not obvious; it needs revealing. No one would have imagined (2:9) that the cross of Christ was the way in which God would reconcile men to himself. This method is certainly not the way of "the rulers of this age." It contrasts sharply with the world's standards of having power and control over others.

The Mind of Christ (2:16)

The wisdom of God that is recognized by the mature is not obvious to men. This is true at two levels. On one hand, the gospel is widely rejected by those who seek wisdom and demand miracles. Most of the world has not believed in the cross because it believes in power not weakness, ruling not serving, self-sufficiency, not dependency.

But at a second level, the word of the cross is difficult even for Christians to fully believe in. The message of the cross is much more than the story of how Jesus met his death, it is the shape of his life and the lives of those who follow him.

The artist Holman Hunt has painted a picture of Jesus working as a boy in Joseph's carpentry shop. As he works, the frame in the window casts a shadow of a cross upon his back. The painting well illustrates how the cross is not a solitary event in Jesus' ministry but the basic stance of his life.

Although it is difficult, most of us can see the truth of the cross-shaped life of Jesus. It is hard to realize that this message is not only about Jesus' ministry. It also applies to those who accept his invitation to "take up your cross and follow him." Whenever we think that our piety or worship or our understandings give us special privileges, we need to become nervous. We are obeying the gospel of a king leading an army against Jerusalem, not the gospel of one who died amidst outlaws outside the city gates, a man of sorrows acquainted with grief.

When Paul says "we have the mind of Christ," many believe he is referring only to himself or to a select few, such as the apostles. This interpretation raises again the distinction between ordinary and extraordinary Christians. There is no doubt that the apostles had a unique and special role in the church's development. However, in view of Paul's concern to stress the equality of members, it is doubtful that in verse 16 he introduces a distinction between the average member and those who attain the mind of Christ.

Similarly, Paul urges in Philippians 2:5 to "have this mind among yourselves, which you have in Christ Jesus." In context we see that Paul is urging Christians not to act from conceit or selfishness but to seek the interests of others (Phil. 2:4). Philippians 2:6-11 describes how Jesus did not claim special privileges but willingly became a servant of men. Because of Jesus' willingness to live humbly and in service to others, God demonstrated his approval by resurrecting Christ and installing him as Lord.

As we keep this in mind and return to 1 Corinthians 2:16, it seems clear that the Corinthians are being urged to stop their petty divisiveness because it is against the mind of Christ, the word of the cross. The really mature Christian is not determined by intellectual ability or a power to speak or teach. The mature man in Christ has come to recognize that Christ has left for his people a pattern of service to one another, not special advantages to compete with.

Back to Basics

I have an interest in photography and have come to know some professional photographers. These men usually prefer to shoot black and white pictures. I began to use black and white film because it was cheaper and because I could learn to develop my own pictures. But I quickly gave up black and white as too unexciting and started using color film. The professionals still use black and white, but they do so with greater skill and understanding. It is more challenging to make a black and white photo exciting than a color shot of flowers.

This is truth we come to very slowly. We became babes in Christ with very limited understanding of some basics—that Jesus was born as God's Son and our Savior, that he lived and taught, that he died on the cross for our forgiveness, and that God raised him from the dead. When we believed these truths we could come to believe in him.

Then we progressed to learning dates and names, recognizing minor Bible characters, and memorizing passages—all appropriate goals. Then we came to understand the great ideas and concepts, searching difficult passages and hard doctrines. That too was a growth step. But to build upon this and move beyond it, we came back to the cross to understand more deeply the style of service that it represents. We learn that the cross does not teach us to think of others first and ourselves second; it teaches us to not consider our own advantage at all. Then we can accept Jesus' own words, "If any one would be first, he must be least of all and servant of all" (Mark 9:35).

Only the mature will come to see this and to imitate the mind of the Master. The foolish message of the cross is a stumbling block to religious people and foolishness to wise people in any age. For the wisdom and piety of the world purport that one becomes successful by getting his way in the world and leaving behind those less significant. The world's wisdom tries to impress God with our knowledge and our religion. It forgets the cross.

Belonging Together

3

1 Corinthians 1:10-17; 3:1-23

Many metropolitan newspapers carry classified housing ads that list apartments for rent to select groups. There are apartments for singles, for young marrieds without children, for retirees, and other special groups. Have you ever thought about how many ways mankind can be divided up into groups? For example, we have racial groups, social classes, economic divisions, and ethnic backgrounds, to name a few.

The question this raises for Christians, both in ancient Corinth and in late twentieth-century America, is whether an understanding of the gospel leads to still other select groups. If life in Christ is a new way to divide humanity, then what "good news" is there in being divided from each other? We see the same dilemma in 1 Corinthians 1 and 2, where the question of the nature of the gospel message and the problem of divisions within the Corinthian church are so closely related.

Divisions Among You (1:10-12)

Jesus warned that a house divided against itself would fall. Although he was speaking of possible revolution in Satan's kingdom, these words are applicable to the church as well. In spite of an excellent beginning by receiving the wisdom of God and the gift of the Spirit, the church at Corinth is divided into competing groups. Paul learned of this from some travelling Christians from Chloe's household (1 Cor. 1:11) and addresses the problem without being asked.

The Corinthians were divided into varying loyalties behind certain prominent church leaders. In 1 Corinthians 1–3 Paul locates the reasons for this factionalism, its basic error, and its effects upon spiritual growth and offers advice for positive relationships to church leaders.

It is depressing to open the yellow pages of a telephone directory and look under *churches*. There we see how men have used their religious commitments to create ways of marking themselves off from other men. Indeed, just from this examination, it is painful to read statements in the New Testament about reconciliation, such as Ephesians 2:14 or Colossians 1:19-20. What has happened to Christian unity?

Paul mentions three men—and Christ too—as being centers for the various factions within the Corinthian church. Whether these were the only groups or if there were still others is unknown. Some of the Corinthians aligned themselves with Paul, others with Cephas (Peter), still others with Apollos. We do not know why these particular men were chosen for the party loyalties. Paul has often been suggested as the one favored by those Christians who emphasized Christ's grace and freedom. Cephas has been regarded as the hero of those who stressed the Jewish heritage of Christianity and perhaps had a greater respect for legal traditions. Apollos has been thought influential because of his skill as a thinker and speaker.

Similar characteristics in men and motivations for cliquishness are found among Christians today. Even within a congregation not threatened by division, there are those who greatly stress their freedom in Christ and others who fear such freedom. Many powerful speakers have been idolized by hearers to the extent that loyalty to Christ was equated with loyalty to the speaker.

Why Are There Factions?

First, factions form because men develop a false loyalty to human leaders. Note that Paul does not favor one faction over another. He does not try to win adherents to the Paul party, or even the Christ party. He uniformly opposes all the cliques. It is *factionalism*, not this or that faction, that Paul opposes.

A second reason for division is man's reliance on human wisdom (1:17). This is the burden of the previous chapter in our study. Human wisdom seeks to honor those who are important, who are powerful or rich or wise. That is why men seek out qualities to laud in individuals, such as Paul's freedom or Peter's dependability or Apollos' speaking ability. If Christians honor human skills and powers, inevitably they will seek out men who have these skills and powers to claim them as the wisest or the most loyal or the best speaker.

Thirdly, divisions within the church are the result of pride. The partisans of Paul, Apollos, and Cephas are not praising their leaders. They are praising themselves. Note that their slogans begin with "*I* belong to . . ." The real object of praise is the "I" (1:12)—the "I" who is wise enough to recognize the greatest leader and become part of his group. In a back-handed way, the Corinthians are praising themselves when they laud prominent church leaders.

Paul's Response

Paul responds to the Corinthian divisiveness in seven ways. First, he begins with three rhetorical questions (1

Cor. 1:13-16). Second, he shows that the wisdom of the cross opposes divisions (1 Cor. 2; see chapter 2 in this book). Third, he discusses evidence of spiritual maturity (3:1-4). Fourth, he sets out the proper way for Christians to regard their leaders (3:5-9). Fifth, he points out that the Corinthians are accountable if they build a faulty church that divides (3:10-15). Sixth, he shows that division is serious, because it destroys God's temple, the church (3:16-17). And seventh, he shows that division is caused by foolish and selfish striving for the riches of God that are ours already (3:18-23).

Three Questions for Partisans (1:13-17)

Is Christ divided? The obvious answer is no. There is only one Christ, one Savior and Lord. The Corinthians made that confession when they first became Christians. They made it in prayers and hymns in their worship. Paul quotes an early Christian hymn or confession in 8:6 that speaks of one Lord and one God. Therefore, it is blasphemous to consider the Savior as parcelled out among Jew and Greek, slave and free.

Was Paul crucified for you? Again the answer is obvious. Although Paul gladly gave himself to be spent for his churches, he did not pay the price of their redemption. Even if Paul were to have imitated the death of the Lord, his crucifixion could never have been redemptive in the way Jesus' death was.

Were you baptized into Paul? The expression "in the name" means "into the authority of" (Matt. 28:19). Paul had no authority to have one baptized in his name.

In some mystery religions of Paul's day a convert felt a special attachment for his instructor who had taught him the mysteries and performed the initiation rites, which often including washings. Perhaps some Corinthians regarded their relationships to Paul in a similar way. Perhaps that is why Paul says he is grateful that he did little baptizing in Corinth and that he can scarcely recall whom he baptized. First Corinthians 1:17 definitely does not imply any disinterest in baptism by Paul. Indeed, when we consider that Paul couples baptism in this passage with Christ and the crucifixion, this verse becomes an impressive support for baptism's importance.

Yet the purpose of verse 17 is not to explain or criticize baptism, but to warn against a party spirit. Paul tactfully uses himself as the example in each case. A party spirit is not just undesirable; it is in contradiction to the death of Christ, the baptism of Christians, and even Christ himself.

These verses have a warning today. The human desire to surround oneself with only those who share our ideas or who share our taste in people or who know and use the right shibboleths is still present. We need to guard against allowing others to find in us a focus for a party spirit. This temptation is hard to resist because it comes disguised as praise of our learning, applause at our lessons, and compliments to our uncompromising ways. What might seem a proper (and enjoyable) recognition of our service can be easily twisted into division within the church—even when the recognition was sincerely given.

The identity of the "Christ party" has been often discussed.[1] Probably some Corinthians believed they had a special relationship with the Savior, which they denied to others. This would fit the claim of some to be "mature" or "perfect." But regardless of the identity of the party, Paul clearly opposes all factionalism within the church, even the group that boasts of a loyalty only to Christ.

Division and Spiritual Maturity (3:1-4)

It is quite common for a college or a church to conduct a workshop or a lecture series on themes such as "Christian maturity" or "spiritual maturity." Have you ever thought about how one measures such maturity?

In our sons' room is a chart marked off in inches where we periodically note their heights. It is hard for parents to see their children growing physically without some such device. We can measure the growth of our children because there are obvious standards, such as feet and inches, that give us some concrete measurement. The Corinthians claimed to be spiritually mature, but how would one know?

After a discussion of the basis for Christian unity in the word of the cross (1:18–2:16), Paul returns to address directly the issue of division. Although some members of the Corinthian church regarded themselves as advanced, mature believers, Paul says that they have used the wrong measurement.

The Corinthians must have been shocked when Paul referred to them as mere babes in Christ and merely ordinary men ("men of the flesh" means human life as lived without faith—3:1-4). Since they accepted Christ the Corinthians have been on milk, not meat, and they still are not weaned. They are babes because of their sectarian, quarrelsome spirit. Then how does one recognize "spiritual men"?

First, "spiritual men" (3:1) are the same as the "mature" (2:6). They can be contrasted with "fleshly men" (2:14). The key is in 3:4: "When one says 'I belong to Paul,' and another, 'I belong to Apollos,' are you not merely men?" Paul is not urging the Corinthians to become angels, but warning them that if they divide into warring cliques and prideful groups, they act as worldly men.

Second, to be spiritually minded contrasts with being "men of the flesh" (3:1). Certainly this does not urge a nonfleshly existence (how would one do that?). Being

34

spiritually minded means one is directed by God's Spirit and does not rely on normal abilities. Compare, for example, Galatians 5:16-26, in which the works of the flesh are contrasted with the fruit of the Spirit. Ordinary human values contradict those of a life renewed by God's Spirit.

Third, two "fleshly" attitudes are specifically mentioned in 3:3—"jealousy and strife." (They are also listed in the works of the flesh in Gal. 5:19.) Ordinary, unredeemed men are jealous of each other and therefore strive against one another. Such behavior is not unusually sinful; it is simply how the world lives. Again, these worldly values contradict how men are taught to live in Christ by following the Spirit.

Division and Role of God's Workers (3:5-9)

Leaders today are not born that way. They are made—and made quickly. Because of the tremendous power and impact of the electronic media, persons can become recognizable almost overnight. A personality can be tailored to fit the criteria from the latest surveys. Advertising sells leaders as well as products.

How can division be avoided that arose because some Christians who relied upon human standards and accepted wisdom created parties around their leaders? In 3:5-9, Paul describes the proper attitude toward Christian unity. In these verses, Paul is saying, "Let me tell you who these men you are aligning yourselves with really are; then you won't use them to be divisive." Church leaders are not lords but servants. Borrowing an agricultural metaphor, Paul says the human works of sowing or watering are not decisive. God alone produces growth (3:7).

To be a "fellow worker" for God is certainly a noble calling, but it is not the most important thing in church life. The field is not the farmer's, but the Creator's (3:9). Just as God's call (1:9) is the very beginning of faith, the continuing growth in faith is God's work as well. He— not the workmen—deserves all the praise. The implication is that Christians are not to divide a church by rallying around different workers of God.

Division and Faulty Church Builders
(3:10-15)

Everyone who thinks seriously about his Christian service is well aware of its inadequacies and failures. Some are due to our own mistakes, some to the actions of others. This is a real concern to church leaders who are deeply involved with their people. When the church does not become all we have worked for, how much of the blame lies with those who led?

Continuing the idea of building, Paul says in 3:10-15 that he laid the best foundation for the church in Corinth. Now he cautions the Corinthians to be careful how they build their church on that foundation. If they build with the faulty material of selfishness and spiritual immaturity, the church will divide. Thus, Paul holds the Corinthians responsible for their divided church.

Paul urges them to build wisely because the quality of their work will be tested. If they have built well, they will be rewarded in judgment. However, if they have built with shoddy materials, they will lose their accomplishment, but God will still save them. This is the reverse of the fact that the apostle cannot take the credit if growth occurs. Hans Conzelmann has stated this concept well:

> The loss of faith means the loss of salvation. On the other hand, unsatisfactory works performed by a Christian as a Christian do not bring his damnation. This is the reverse side of the fact that our works do not bring about salvation.[2]

Division Destroys God's Temple (3:16-17)

One cannot climb the rocky steps up the Acropolis in Athens and stand before the Parthenon or the Erechtheum without being awed by either structure's timeless beauty. Even photos of these ancient temples are inspiring. In order to understand the comparison of the church and the temple in 3:16-17, it is important to know some facts about the design and function of Greek temples.

Greek and Roman temples were not the pagan equivalents of our church buildings. A temple was not designed for congregational assembly but served as a house in which the idol or god resided. Unlike the Parthenon, most were quite small.

Three designations were used to describe temples. One term, *temenos*, referred to all the sacred site, building and grounds included. Another, *hierion*, referred to the building as a whole (as in our expression "church building"). Yet another word, *naos*, referred to a small inner room within the temple where the image of the pagan god stood. *Naos* is the word Paul uses here to describe Christians as God's temple. We are that "inner sanctuary" where the Deity himself resides. What a magnificent thought that the God of heaven and earth abides within the people called by his name—not in temples made with human hands and by human skills!

Another insight from antiquity gives additional meaning to the concept of the temple as a building. One of the most infamous crimes to the ancients was to desecrate a temple. In fact, one writer describes such acts as madness. Because of this belief, the Greeks and Romans wrote a number of inscriptions and laws that make clear such an action carried the death punishment. Paul applies this attitude to a much more important matter.

If men who physically damage structures made of stone and gold are subject to a death sentence, what shall happen to those who damage the temple of God—his people? Here we see how serious is the matter of party divisions in the church, although the Corinthians had not divided into different congregations that withheld fellowship from each other.

Division and Possessing God's Blessings
(3:18-23)

First Corinthians 3 is not meant to be solely negative and reproaching. There are real blessings in Christ, and they are mediated to us through men. "All things are yours, whether Paul or Apollos or Cephas . . ." If Christian leaders are valued as gifts for mutual upbuilding and not divisiveness, they are genuine blessings.

Because of human wisdom, the Corinthians had misunderstood the cross. They competed against each other for the best leaders, the best gifts, the best spirituality. There was no need for strife. These blessings are already given to those who live for others, not to those who selfishly seek God's blessings. Those who rightly understand the word of the cross—that service is the road to true greatness and that human prestige is unimportant in divine evaluation—have found their place to belong in the church.

---

[1] Carl Holladay, *The First Letter of Paul to the Corinthians* (Austin, Texas: Sweet Publishing Company, 1979), p. 29f.

[2] Hans Conzelmann, *1 Corinthians* (Philadelphia: Fortress, 1977), p. 77. Used by permission.

Judging Our Judging

4

1 Corinthians 4:1-21

One can almost predict the topic of conversation at most offices each Monday during the fall and winter. "Monday morning quarterbacks" gather around the coffee tables to relive and replay the college and professional football games from the weekend. It is one of the favorite American pastimes. People who have no training in coaching and no first-hand knowledge of the abilities or conditions of the players and who, in many cases, have never played even high school football do not hesitate to assess each play called, its execution, and the intelligence of every player!

This is a harmless, if futile, entertainment. The fans feel closer to the game, and surely coaches are unconcerned about having their abilities evaluated in this way. However, this pastime illustrates the human tendency to judge others and assess their achievements and even their worth. Unfortunately, this habit frequently spills over into the church's life as well. In spite of the Lord's warning not to become judges (Matt. 7:1), the Corinthian Christians were busily engaged in evaluating one another. Many modern-day Christians follow the Corinthians' example.

Evaluating God's Servants (4:1-5)

The Corinthians who wanted to establish themselves as "spiritual men" tended quite naturally to evaluate the spirituality of their brethren. Indeed, one of the common ways to inflate one's own status is to downgrade others. The Corinthians had probably devalued Paul (he seems defensive in 1 Cor. 9). However, because the Corinthians had accepted the wisdom of the world rather than the word of the cross as their standard, their judgments were unreliable.

The proper way to view leaders is to regard them as "servants" and "stewards" of God for the benefit of the church (4:1-2). The word translated "servant" referred to men who rowed large ships in antiquity. These ships had on each side two or three levels of oarsmen, who usually were slaves chained in the dark, dangerous hold. The rowers on the bottom level—the most dangerous and uncomfortable level—were the "underrowers," the word here rendered "servants."

"Steward" was used to describe one who was in charge of managing a household for an absent landlord. Very often these stewards were trusted slaves. In Luke 16:1-8, Jesus tells the story of such a steward, who had been irresponsible in his duty and scrambled in fear as the return of the owner was anticipated.

Apostles, like these other workers, were required to be trustworthy. In other words, apostles did not work for themselves; they were responsible for the work of Christ, which they assisted. The same is true for Christians today. Their calling is fulfilled if they treat the trust in a worthy manner, just as God is trustworthy (1 Cor. 1:9; 10:13).

God Will Judge in His Time

Paul makes three points concerning the Corinthian

practice of judging: (1) Christians are not assigned evaluation jobs because that task belongs to God (4:4); (2) any judgment before the Judgment Day is premature (4:5); and (3) we are not competent even to judge ourselves (4:4).

Judgment belongs to God. Although in 1 Corinthians Paul at first appears to be defending himself from a Corinthian censor, this is probably not the case. The Corinthians, unlike the Judaizers Paul faced in Romans 3:8 and Galatians 2:15-21 were more inclined to exercise their freedom by such acts as eating sacrificial meat, allowing women to lead public worship, and even tolerating flagrant immorality. Therefore, it is not likely that some criticized Paul for his preaching of grace. Rather, they judged those believers in Corinth who did not see things as they did.

Paul says he is unconcerned about what evaluation the "spiritual" Corinthians, or any other group places on him. Such judgments are meaningless and are even against the gospel. It is not for one brother to judge the servant of another (Rom. 14:4). Judgment belongs to God.

I do not judge myself. Ours is an introspective age. Self-improvement courses and books challenge us to be more assertive, physically fit, and better organized. Such clichés as "getting in touch with myself" and "discover myself" show how much we are interested in personal examination. If we approach our spiritual lives with such examination, we will likely end up with two results. First, our pride will increase if, like the Corinthians, we are confident that we will pass the course with high honors. Such pride stands in the way of real spiritual growth, for it leaves people "puffed up."

Second, as conscientious people, we are likely to condemn ourselves unreasonably for not attaining perfection. In George Orwell's *Animal Farm*, the only animal who really works after the animals take over the farm is the mule. Although worn out, whenever some problem arises, the mule takes the blame and resolves to himself, "I will work harder."

Many churches have a number of members who have either become neurotic with self-examination and thus are unable to help others or who have so overcommitted their spiritual lives that they burn out and become "pew packers." Both need to realize that neither our own sense of innocence nor the judgment of others—favorable or negative—is important.

Before the time. The Corinthians' self-judgment is also premature. God has "fixed a day on which he will judge the world" (Acts 17:31), but that day has not yet arrived. The correct verdict will come from the court in which God is the judge, and that court has not yet gone into session. God's judgment is reliable because he knows the truth about each of us in a way that others cannot. Jesus once watched a poor woman cast two coins into an offering and pronounced her the greatest giver of the day. This evaluation would not have been obvious to others who watched. Viewed objectively, she did not give much. But her gift was significant above the other gifts because her motive was grander, something observers could not know.

So today when we look over our congregations and decide who is most important, our judgments may not accord with God's. Because it is so hard to know one's motives and private acts, we regard as most important those with a high visibility. Yet the accuracy of such assessments is known only to God and will be revealed only on the last day.

The Judgment Day is usually preached as warning to those who are negligent in their Christian walk. Paul discusses it in this light in 2 Corinthians 5:10. But in 1

Corinthians 4:5 Paul says we are to expect commendation—not judgment—from God on the last day! The point is that all judgment, and even acquittal, are not appropriate now for they belong to the end and to God.

Pride Causes Judging (4:6)

Although Paul has used himself as an example in 4:1-5, in verse 6 he tells us that these instructions are meant for the Corinthians. He is not trying to vindicate himself, but attempting to teach the Corinthians who were busy parading their spiritual verdicts. The purpose of such comparisons between Paul and the Corinthians was so that "none of you may be puffed up in favor of one against another" (4:6). An inflated self-estimate was behind the practice of judging others at Corinth.

The little word "puffed up"(*phusioō*) occurs only seven times in the New Testament, six of which are in 1 Corinthians. Although egoism is a problem in all places, clearly it seems to have been especially prominent in Corinth. The Corinthians are characterized as people too inflated in their speech (4:18-19) and their wisdom (8:1). Even in the midst of extreme moral failure, their self-inflation continued (5:2). This attitude directly contrasts with an attitude of love (13:4).

Paul offers two reasons the Corinthians should not be proud: (1) all they have is a gift; and (2) they have a false sense of perfection.

Gifts Disallow Pride (4:7)

In rebuke of their self-estimate of superiority, Paul ironically asks in 4:7, "Who sees anything different in you?" Or, as a paraphrase renders, "Who in the world sees anything special in you?"

Occasionally some 14 year old who is a true genius with an I.Q. over 150 will appear on a TV talk show.

That such a person would take pride in his I.Q. is not only unpleasant but even foolish. An I.Q. is not an achievement but a gift just as height, beauty, and other characteristics are gifts. These gifts say nothing about one's merits or development. There is no occasion for one to be proud of what has been freely given him.

The Corinthians prided themselves on their possession of spiritual gifts (see chapter 10 of this book). They failed to see that these abilities were not grounds for personal pride, but divine gifts for mutual benefit. In his giving, God places highest value on the humble, a truth the Corinthians failed to grasp (12:24; see also 1 Peter 5:5 and James 4:6).

This problem of pride in our God-given abilities still exists. One finds himself praised as a teacher or preacher or song leader and then begins to enjoy this praise and to compare his talents with others. The snare of pride often comes clothed in Christian garments, but it is not in line with the gospel. Each time Christians begin to congratulate themselves on their spirituality, they need to recall that whatever they have is a gift. Therefore, any praise is due God alone, who gives the gift and who can remove it.

Lack of Perfection Cancels Pride (4:8-13)

One writer has described the Corinthians as "overconverted." They emphasized only the present in Christian living and had little expectation for the future. They believed their spiritual gifts, especially speaking in tongues, were proof they were completely mature. Their false sense of perfection made them proud.

In interpreting 1 Corinthians 4:8-13, one must recognize the irony Paul uses in his caricatures of the Corinthians' inflated self-estimation. When he says the Corinthians are "rich" and "filled," he does not really believe that this is the case. This is clear from his remark in verse 8, "Would that you did reign, so that we might share your rule!" In essence, he asks rhetorically, "How did it happen that you Corinthians are already on the thrones of heaven and we poor apostles who taught you still suffer?"

Notice how the Corinthians are contrasted with Paul and the other apostles. The apostles are fools; the Corinthians are wise. The apostles are weak; the Corinthians are strong. The apostles are disreputable; the Corinthians are honored. (The Jerusalem Bible says, "You are celebrities; we are nobodies.") These passages continue the contrasts of the gospel and human wisdom in 1 Corinthians 1. Paul noted in 1:26 that the people of God are not the worldly wise; they are the weak and foolish who lack status. In this way the community of faith reflects the character of the gospel.

Perfectionism Versus the Cross

The form of perfectionism that developed in Corinth has been described as a "theology of glory." It stresses the achievements and attainments of those in Christ, as well as their spirituality, their heavenly worship, and their exalted station before God. This understanding of Christianity leaves the cross behind in the rush for glory. Such perfectionism may be caricatured as "*Theirs* is the kingdom, the power and the glory." The Corinthians found proof of this glory in their wisdom, the Lord's Supper, and especially spiritual gifts.

Like most aberrations of the Christian faith, the "theology of glory" has some truth in it. Christians presently have magnificent gifts from God—salvation, hope, love, the Spirit, access to God in prayer, and freedom from guilt. We have been washed, sanctified, and justified (6:11).

Again Paul compares the word of the cross with the Corinthian-glorified Christianity, which espouses only a successful life in the present. The basic assumption of the Corinthians is wrong—that to be a mature Christian is to have it good. Christianity is not a baptized success ethic in which Jesus is a patron of getting ahead. The Corinthians overlook the word of the cross, which speaks not of angels in glory but of one who, in humility, sought the benefit of others.

Forgetting the cross in the Christian message is a danger today, too. TV preachers assure us that Jesus wants us to be a success, and "born again" celebrities tell us that their careers prospered when they accepted Jesus. In the push to get to the resurrection, many a sermon has neglected the cross. The word of the cross is still the same—a service to others and abandonment of one's own gains.

Paul's chastened view of church leaders in 1 Corinthians 4:9 is poignantly described by a metaphor from Roman civic life. A general who returned from a foreign victory would be honored by the Roman government with a parade in the city. He would lead the parade in his golden chariot, surrounded by children carrying incense and throwing flowers. Behind him in splendid array would be the victorious army in dress uniform. Behind the soldiers were the spoils of war—gold, art, jewels, and similar wealth. At the end of the parade were the vanquished captives. After the parade the captives would enter the arena to fight gladiators and wild animals for the right to live.

Using this example, Paul suggests if the Corinthians are the great and honored men leading the parade and receiving praise for their wisdom and spirituality, he and other apostles are like the condemned men at the end who are to be killed in the arenas. What a strange irony!

It is clear which part of the parade is modeled upon the cross.

A friend has a wall plaque which proclaims, "Christians aren't perfect, just forgiven." This could be understood in two ways. It could mean either, "Although we are not perfect, as Christians we are nevertheless forgiven by God." Or it could mean, "In this life we Christians do not attain perfection and should not expect to do so, even though we are really forgiven." Both of these interpretations summarize the point of 1 Corinthians 4.

Who Can Speak Thus? (4:14-15)

Most of us will honestly admit that we don't take criticism very well. We may have one or two very close friends from whom we can accept a rebuke, but even then we feel a twinge of defensiveness. When Paul brings his rebuke to a close, he pauses to remind the Corinthians both of his right to speak so frankly and his motive for doing so.

Paul's right to be frank is rooted in his close relationship with the church. He is their father in the gospel (cf. Gal. 4:19 and 1 Thess. 2:11 for similar imagery). Surely a father has both the right and obligation to be concerned about his children and to speak freely with them. In verse 15 Paul's father relationship is contrasted with that of "guides." The word "guide" refers to a household slave who was responsible for watching small children, seeing them safely to their destinations, and protecting them from any dangers. This was a great responsibility and was given to the most trusted slave in the house. Nevertheless, his concern for his charges could never equal that of their father. Because of his paternal relationship, Paul can admonish the Corinthians, urge their imitation of him, and discipline them.

Imitate Your Father (4:16-17)

I have often known people who thought the goal of Christian education was to acquire knowledge. This is not the goal; it is only a means. The real goal is to shape the life of the learner in accordance with the gospel. A full knowledge and mature wisdom may be a necessary step, but it is not the goal of education.

Paul recognizes this when he says that he sends Timothy to teach "my ways." The greatest tool for teaching others is the combination of a good knowledge of Christian doctrine and a life conformed to its demands. The combination of teaching and deeds gives what is most impressive to others—integrity. That is why Paul wants the Corinthians to know not only what he teaches informationally, but how he lives in Christ.

Similarly, we can believe and follow Jesus because he had integrity. If we discovered that Jesus had gone to his death crying for mercy from Pilate and offering to stop teaching, we would be able to understand that from a humanly standpoint. Before accepting death, most of us would consider limiting our ideals. However, if that had happened, Jesus' words would lack integrity. Regardless of his fate, Jesus' great parables and sayings would be just as true but markedly less believable.

Too often we have contrasted those who had right knowledge with those who did good deeds, as if these were two options. Paul combines both the message and the deeds in his life. The integrity of a message about a cross and a cross-shaped life would be a believable sign in our time.

Heed Fatherly Discipline (4:18-21)

Like other parents, Paul knows that his concern may be disregarded and his instructions ignored, despite his deep personal concern for the Corinthians' welfare.

Therefore, he concludes by telling rebellious children who believe that Paul is all talk and no action that although he prefers to come with love and gentleness, he can also exercise his obligation to discipline his children.

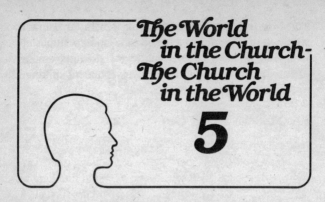

The World
in the Church-
The Church
in the World

5

1 Corinthians 5:1–6:20

In some Christian art of the third and fourth centuries the church is pictured as a small boat with a cross-shaped mast. The boat is storm-tossed amid mighty waves. This imagery portrays well the aspect of the church as a refuge to its surrounding culture. Another image—this one more difficult to portray visually—is Jesus' description of the church as preserving salt for the world (Matt. 5:13). In this image the church is a saving ingredient mixed in with the world. Both images are correct, and the tension between them is creative, not contradictory. These images give us clues about how to live in the world.

It has always been a problem for Christians to live faithfully to the Lord who calls us, yet responsibly in the world in which we are called. To fulfill its purpose the church cannot retreat from the world into holy isolation. Yet involvement with the world often results in Christians accepting the world's standards rather than those of their Master. Paul addresses this problem in 1 Corinthians 5 and 6.

Beginning in chapter 5 Paul takes up a series of practical questions about the relationship of Christians to the world. In these two chapters he deals with three moral problems in Corinth: (1) a notoriously sinful relationship of incest (5:1-8), (2) the matter of lawsuits among Christians (6:1-11), and (3) the involvement of some Christians with prostitutes (6:12-20).

Keeping the World Out (5:1-8)

Although the world generally sits pretty loose regarding some sins (lying, petty theft, eroticism), there are some evils even a jaded secular world would find hard to understand. First Corinthians 5:1-8 discusses such a case, which involved a Christian man who had an incestuous relationship with his "father's wife" (presumably his stepmother, since there is a clear Greek word for mother).

Details of this sinful relationship are unknown to us, perhaps because Paul knew they were common knowledge in Corinth! Or perhaps he was too embarrassed to repeat them in a letter. Nevertheless, the blatant character of this sin was particularly offensive and dangerous to the Christian community. Yet this sinful relationship was not only known but condoned—either explicitly or implicitly—among the church members (5:2)! Paul expresses two concerns about this problem in 1 Corinthians 5. First, Christian conduct has fallen to what even the pagan world deems a low standard. Second, and more far-reaching, the Corinthians lack proper remorse for this situation.

The world seeps in. Although such illicit relationships were condemned by pagan law, society in the first century was clearly known for sexual looseness. Pagans tended to view sexuality as natural, to be enjoyed in the same way as eating (note the slogans quoted in 6:12, 13), that is, as often and as varied as one might want. Pagans opposed infidelity in marriage not because it was immoral but because it meant the mate was unreliable.

Corinth's reputation as the most wicked of cities and the story of its 1,000 sacred prostitutes of Aphrodite probably arose from Athenian propaganda. However, because such charges persisted, they are generally regarded as correct assessments of the city. Indeed, one might expect such morality in a seaport city, especially a newly built one where adventurers and fortune seekers often came and where family ties were lacking. It would be hard—especially for recently converted pagans—to avoid the lowest levels of morals in such a cosmopolitan city as Corinth.

Obviously, the church in twentieth-century America is in a similar situation. Sexual immorality has always existed, and its evil influence has always drawn some Christians astray. In our time, however, loose sexual morals are no longer hidden or apologized for; they are openly promoted. Prominent people appear on TV talk shows to discuss their latest "arrangements," and autobiographies give the details and assessments of the authors' affairs. Even the fiction of repeated marriage and divorce ("serial bigamy") that once disguised such illicit relationships is no longer felt necessary. Indeed, the sexual revolution that accepts such morality is so prevalent that we need not argue the point.

Like the Corinthians, our problem is how to face the challenge when the morals of the pagan culture invade the church. As heirs of Greek ethics, the Corinthians were individualists in moral matters. Each person was allowed—even encouraged—to decide his own morality. His decisions were regarded as a private concern. Morality was not a community concern. Like the Corinthian church, the church today is surrounded by similar individualism in ethical matters.

Since the "Me-decade" of the 1970's, morality has

widely come to be regarded as a private rather than public matter. The church has heard the culture's individualism in such slogans as "I've got to be me" and "I did it my way." Not surprisingly, many Christians have been influenced to accept such individualism of morals.

Removing worldliness. The first part of a strategy to improve Christian morality is to decide that the church does have a stake in the personal morals of members. This is really the focus of Paul's outrage; the Corinthians remain proud in a situation where it would be more fitting to be in mourning, as over one dead in sin (5:2)! Then, when the expressed concern of the church fails to correct such sin, steps must be taken to discipline the member who persists in sin. This approach actually follows Jesus' instructions (Matt. 18:15-17). The discipline discussed in 1 Corinthians 5 is exclusion from the church, including the fellowship of the table (5:11). Three things should be noted about this exclusion.

First, it is not retribution but discipline. The goal is not to punish the offender, but to restore his salvation (5:5). In my youth I witnessed a disfellowshipping. Although I cannot remember the details, I do recall that a great deal of anger and resentment was directed at the man. Such attitudes suggest the motives for the discipline were not the best.

Second, for church discipline to be effective in restoring the wayward, there must be some fellowship to withdraw from the person! In a cold, faceless, impersonal world, the warmth of genuine Christian fellowship can bring meaning and significance to life. When Christians are deeply involved in the lives of one another, the removal of such a support system is a significant loss.[1] Such deep involvement does not just happen. It has to be planned for and nurtured in the church just as it should be in the biological family.

Third, the exclusion is for the protection of the rest of the church. Likening the church to the Passover celebration with Christ as the paschal lamb, Paul urges them to cast out the old leaven of sin so that they may be unpolluted (5:6-8).

As an example of how such church discipline should work, Paul tells the Corinthians "not to eat" with the offender. It is unclear whether he means not to share in the Lord's Supper or not to partake a meal with the man. Perhaps he means both. Through this Paul indirectly gives us a clue on how to develop positive fellowship—by sharing meals. Our forefathers used such "dinners on the grounds" as an excellent way to promote fellowship. The most loved minister in my memory of my home congregation often planned—and sometimes cooked!—church dinners.

As churches have become much larger, however, even the "church picnic" has become somewhat ineffective for cultivating personal involvement among believers. Many churches have arranged home gatherings for meals by dividing their congregation into smaller units for Christian nurture. A private home opened to others is more likely to provide an atmosphere of meaningful fellowship than a church building.

Keeping the Church In (5:9-13)

Moving beyond the immediate problem of church discipline, Paul turns to consider the proper relationship of the church to the world. This relationship is based on the principle that the church should have a concerned, disciplined life among its members and a loving acceptance of those without it.

It is possible that the statement, "If we are not to associate with the immoral, we will have to get out of the world," was argued by some confused about Paul's instructions. However, since Paul makes it clear elsewhere (1 Cor. 8, for example) that the Corinthians had not dropped out of society, it is likely that such an objection is insincere. In actuality, the Corinthians sought to justify their desire to live as their pagan neighbors.

In 1 Corinthians 5 Paul states explicitly that Christians are not permitted to withdraw from the larger society to pursue their lives in solitude. We may be amused or impressed with such groups as the Amish who seek to avoid this sinful world. But Paul says that Christians are not to take the path of dissociation, despite its obvious allure as we find an increasingly hostile world. Monasticism, whether in the 12th or 20th century, perverts the center of the gospel, which proclaims that God actively seeks the sinful world rather than shuns it. The gospel is not about how nice things are in heaven; rather, it tells of the Man from heaven who left it to seek the good of his Father's enemies.

The last two verses capsulize the point of 1 Corinthians 5. Christians are to have a community in which the moral standards of the world are not only met but exceeded. This demand requires that the church not regard sins as only a private matter, but also as a concern of the whole community.

Towards those who do not share our stance Christians are not to be judgmental but caring. The world is very accustomed to the church throwing rocks at the sinful, but too seldom does it see the church bandaging the wounded along the wreck-strewn roads of life. We cannot present the church as an ideal community to which sinners may come after they have cleaned up their lives! The world lacks the spiritual resources (God's grace, prayer, the Spirit, the support of brethren) to affect a change of life on its own. If the world could be upright on its own, it would not need a Savior.

Going to Court (6:1-6)

The second question of moral conduct involves Christians going to public courts against one another. Some Christians were taking fellow believers to court over "matters pertaining to this life" (6:3). Once again, the details are not given but were commonly known to both Paul and the Corinthians.

To appreciate this situation, we must understand how much Greeks loved to go to court. Because they were so proud of the free access to courts, Greeks tended to regard lawsuits almost as a pastime. It was the favorite means to exhibit one's speaking skills and ability to form and win an argument. This custom explains why the Corinthian Christians may have continued going to court over matters after their conversion.

However, Jewish people disdained the use of pagan courts. They preferred to have a man of repute within the Jewish community as judge, even if he lacked legal authority. Two reasons are suggested for this. First, pagan courts involved oaths to pagan gods that Jews regarded as idolatrous. Second, the Jewish emphasis on the community tended to place first what was best for the whole people. Again we see that Greek individualism in Corinth was in conflict with the Bible's stress on community.

Paul presents several reasons why Christians should not go to court before pagans. First, Christians are to judge the world and even angels (6:2-3). Exactly what this involves is not stated. The interest is not on such future judging but on the relative contrast between the future role of Christians in judging and their taking trivial matters to pagan courts. If Christians are to judge heavenly beings, how is it that they cannot decide much less important "matters of business" (NEB).

Paul also advises against going to pagan courts because, by doing so, the Corinthians sought the decisions of those for which they had little esteem (6:4-6). The Corinthians, as we have seen, were very proud of their wisdom and knowledge. Perhaps with some sarcasm Paul asks, "Isn't there *one* wise Christian among you 'wise' Corinthians who could settle disputes?" The Jerusalem Bible puts this well: "Is there really not one reliable man among you?"

Better Be Wronged Than Wrong (6:7-8)

The real point of this discussion is revealed in 6:7-8. Paul is not trying to set up a Christian court system at all. In this matter, he differs from Judaism, which established a court system for internal regulations. Rather, Paul says that running to court over matters of daily life shows that the Corinthians have failed to grasp even the most basic truth of the gospel of the cross—why not suffer wrong rather than to wrong others?

Here it becomes clear that what appears as a minor ethical problem about lawsuits among Christians is really a matter of a correct understanding of the gospel. When a Christian insists on his rights and prosecutes others to obtain these rights, he fails to perceive what the gospel message has told us. Throughout the letter Paul reminds Christians that the gospel doesn't bring us privileges but opportunities to serve as the Master did. Just as Jesus renounced his privileges for our benefit (cf. Phil. 2:5-11), so we are to renounce our claims, rather than harm others. To sue another Christian over "things of this life" is evidence that the gospel has not been effective. Why trot this failure into the public courts?

This principle is probably no easier to follow today than it was in the first century. There has been much discussion on whether Christians today are allowed to sue and whom. But the intent of Paul's concern is much sharper than this specific offense. The real issue is how we regard others in view of Christ's example of giving up his rights. In many cases, lawsuits are really matters of ego, with one person seeking to prove his ability to defeat another. Such a practice misreads the gospel of reconciliation through suffering for others.

The Way We Were (6:9-11)

Picking up on the idea of "wronging" in 6:7-8, Paul pauses to remind Christians of their own transformation. ("Unrighteous" in 6:9 is the same word in the Greek as "wrong" in 6:7-8.) People who would wrong others rather than risk losing something have forgotten their conversion. The Corinthians used to be deeply involved in all that it meant to live a worldly life, not just lawsuits but also immoral sex, theft, drunkenness, and greed (perhaps an allusion to the motive of their lawsuits). But in Christ the Corinthians—and Christians today—are done with all that malice.

These three verses are a graphic testimony to the power of the gospel to change human life. Jesus can change people's lives from those that are described in verses 9 and 10. In our experience we may have difficulty believing this because we seldom see people of such backgrounds converted. This is partly because we seldom approach these people with the gospel; we may secretly doubt they can be changed! Yet these verses show otherwise.

Sexuality Is Spiritual (6:12-20)

The third moral issue faced in Corinth is a more common sexual problem than the specific case of the man and his father's wife. Some Corinthians were apparently frequenting prostitutes and justifying this practice on the grounds that such sexual relations were as natural as eating. They believed that just as part of man was made for digestion, another part was made for sexual relations, and both were permissible.

Paul actually quotes two arguments from the Corinthians. "All things are lawful for me" (6:12), and "Food is meant for the stomach and the stomach for food" (6:13). He refutes these arguments with two reminders. First, even some things that are "lawful" are not automatically good. Christianity is not a matter of being unrestrained but of having self-control. Even good things can be perverted when they enslave men (cf. Rom. 6:15-18). Second, all of life, including bodily functions, is accountable to God, and God did not create the body for sin but for the Lord (6:13). A parallel argument is found in Romans 14:17, "The kingdom of God does not mean food and drink but righteousness and peace and joy in the Holy Spirit."

Because Greek philosophy separated man into physical and spiritual halves, it tended to regard the physical as unfit and unable to have religious importance. Moreover, the Greek view that whatever was natural was good made both gluttony and profligacy acceptable to some. Both were only "physical" and did not touch the "spiritual" man.

Although some materialists would reduce man to only an upright animal, most people see a greater significance in humanity. However, those who have considered man's spiritual significance too often limit it to only the invisible life. Public ethics are widely regarded as less important for religious faith than internal feeling or beliefs.

The real revolutionary character of Christian ethics is nowhere better expressed than in Paul's insistence that "the body is . . . for the Lord and the Lord for the body" (6:13). It would be almost inconceivable to a pagan Greek that one could "glorify God in your body" (6:20) or that one's "body is a temple of the Holy Spirit" (6:19). By overcoming this distinction between spiritual and physical, Christianity rejects the idea that there is a nonreligious side of life. All life is religious—or irreligious.

This principle is important for a recovery of Christian living. Just as our Lord really became flesh and dwelt among us, so our fleshly bodies are useful for his spiritual service. "Present your *bodies* as a living sacrifice" (Rom. 12:1). This has important implications for life today. First, Christians are mistaken when they tend to regard physical acts, such as benevolence, as less "spiritual" than nonphysical acts, such as prayer. Jesus indicates in Matthew 25 that benevolence is just as significant as prayer or preaching in deciding our destiny. Second, this passage reminds us that no part of our lives is our own and doesn't involve the Lord. "You have been bought and paid for" (6:20, JB).

---

[1]For an excellent discussion of Christians' needs to become deeply involved in each other's lives, see James Thompson, *Our Life Together* (Austin, Texas: Sweet Publishing Company, 1977).

Grow Where You Are Planted

6

1 Corinthians 7:1-40

Many people today seem to live by the popular song "Somewhere Over the Rainbow" from the film classic *The Wizard of Oz*. For although there are very few places left in the United States that are open to homesteaders, the frontier experience has influence even today. Many people still pull up their families and move to a location where they have never been and where they have no assurance of work, confident that in so doing they will find the pot of gold.

A similar belief is held by some in spiritual matters. Many Christians think that because they are unable to grow spiritually where they are and are not really useful to God in their present situation, in other places they would be more spiritual. Of course, it is true that we are affected by circumstances, and some people do better in some situations than others. However, we can not advance our acceptability to God by changing our situation. In 1 Corinthians 7 Paul addresses the desire to change one's spirituality by changing surroundings.

What Was the Question?

Have you ever been in a room while someone else was talking on the telephone? It is an interesting experience.

Even if the person talking is secretive, you can get a good idea of what is being said on the other end of the line.

The reader of 1 Corinthians 7 experiences a similar situation. Beginning with this chapter, Paul takes up some questions that the Corinthians had asked him. We do not have their letter, but from Paul's reply we can reconstruct the Corinthians' questions with some confidence, especially since Paul seems to quote from their letter in places.

In chapter 7 the topic is married life and related questions. First Corinthians 7:1 appears to contain a quotation from the Corinthians, "It is well for a man not to touch a woman." These words can scarcely be Paul's, for he goes on to argue for married life including sexual relations. Where did the Corinthians get this viewpoint?

The most probable source of a negative view of marriage is Greek philosophy, where certain teachers argued against men being involved with women because the teachers had a highly negative view of the body and its functions. Unlike the Bible, which proclaims that creation is good, many Greek thinkers believed that only the invisible spirit/soul of man was good and the flesh was evil. It would be understandable if some Gentile Christians carried over this attitude into their own lives and tried to encourage a Christian celibacy. Indeed, they might have appealed to Paul as an example!

Today Christian leaders are not likely to argue for congregational celibacy on the grounds that sex is physical and therefore evil. However, there have been times when Christians have been doubtful about the goodness of sex and when this God-designed relationship between husband and wife has been considered only slightly acceptable. In his book *The Corinthian Church*, Bill Baird comments, "When Christians talk about sex, if they ever do, they usually express one of two or three common views. The first is ascetic; the less said about sex the better."[1] Thankfully, this negative, unbiblical attitude is widely refuted today, although there is some danger of Christians overreacting and being drawn into the "sex-ploitation" common to modern American life.

In the first seven verses of 1 Corinthians 7 Paul stakes out some basic attitudes Christians ought to have toward married life. These are as important for us as for the Corinthians, even if we do not share their philosophy. Our culture too is preoccupied with sexuality, in part a result of our high mobility and rootlessness.

First, clearly we are taught that marriage and the sexual aspect of it are "good." "Good" does not simply mean pleasurable, but approved by God, in the same sense that God pronounces his creation "good" after creating male and female (Gen.1:31).

Second, Christian married life is to be complete with a sexual relationship. Indeed, Paul sounds very modern when he argues that both husband and wife have equal rights in this matter. For one partner to try to forbid this relationship is fraud (7:3-5).

Third, Christian couples are permitted to forego marital relations under three conditions: (1) both partners agree, (2) they abstain only for a prescribed time so that abstinence does not become a new life-style, and (3) they devote themelves to prayer while they are abstaining, thus performing a type of fasting.

From this basic discussion on married life, the rest of the chapter continues to take up selected cases: the unmarried and widows (7:8-9), married Christians considering divorce (7:10-11), marriage between a Christian and a non-Christian (7:12-16), and the unmarried who have planned marriage (7:25-38). Verses 17-24 is really the major focus of 1 Corinthians 7 and will receive a special consideration in this chapter.

Where Were You When Called? (7:17-24)

Because the issues described in 1 Corinthians 7 are very concrete ones and related directly to specific situations, there is a temptation to think that they have little to say to us unless we are considering either marriage or divorce. Indeed this chapter is widely regarded as Paul's essay on marriage! Yet this interpretation seems to be only a very surface reading of this chapter. The real message of the chapter has much to teach us apart from the questions about marriage.

We have already considered the concept of being a called people (see chapter 1) and that concept recurs here. By "called" the New Testament does not mean a process of sorting out humanity into two stacks. "Called" refers to the priority of God's work in Christ to save men. The gospel began with God before men heard it.

When asked by the Corinthians whether they should marry or not marry, what answer does Paul give? He seems to be confused. On the one hand, he stresses the benefits of his own situation as an unmarried man. On the other, he insists that marriage is God-ordained and an approved life also. Is it that he approves both marriage and single living? Yes, but more than that. He *disapproves* Christians trying to improve their spiritual status by radically altering who they are—specifically who they were when they answered the divine invitation of the gospel. His answer—stated in 7:17, 24—is to remain as we were when called.

The summons not to seek to improve our situation before God by a change in life situation is well illustrated by Paul's words about circumcision or slavery (7:18-23). These social situations—like marriage—are shown to be irrelevant in our acceptability to God. They thereby illustrate his teaching about marriage to remain in our call.

Because verses 17 and 24 substantially repeat themselves, they serve as brackets to the central discussion of 1 Corinthians 7—remaining as we were "when called." This refers to one's situation of life when first believing in Christ. Specifically in terms of Corinth, this concept relates to marriage. Some apparently felt that being celibate was a more acceptable spiritual position. Thus some who were married were seeking divorce from their mates (7:10-16). Divorce was especially attractive to those with pagan spouses who might have ridiculed or limited their Christian activities. It would be understandable if some felt they could serve Christ better without this hindrance.

The unmarried felt it mandatory to remain single and to break off any engagements (7:25-28). Paul agrees that single living may be easier, but he disagrees that it is more acceptable to God (vs. 28). He regards being single as a practical advantage, specifically a divine gift (7:7).

Finally, some in Corinth felt they could be more spiritual if, as married persons, they eliminated the sexual aspect of the marriage relationship (7:3-5). Paul regards this as both foolish and wrong.

Accepting Our Own Calling

Today there are some who feel that they would be more acceptable to God if only they had married differently. Their marriage, they believe, is the real hindrance in their spiritual life, and, if it were changed, God would prize them more and they would mature as Christians.

It would be foolish to deny that some marriages are more supportive of Christian principles than others. Some do live in situations that require unending patience to endure goading, jibes, and occasional abuse because the spouse resents the believer's commitment. Marriages are not the same everywhere, and they do greatly affect one's spiritual life.

Nevertheless, it is important to realize that Christian commitment is no less acceptable to God because of one's marriage. God holds no grudges about one's marriage—even if that person may hold some regrets. God is pleased to have his men or women where they are. He knows of everyone's efforts and limits in ways that others do not.

But the message of growing where you are planted has significance beyond the specific issue of marriage. Many—perhaps most—people feel that they would be more useful and acceptable to God if only they were in a different situation. This is the *Wizard of Oz* faith mentioned at the beginning of this chapter. Such a faith always keeps looking over some rainbow for a place to be a Christian.

Many think like this: If only I lived in a different city or in a different neighborhood. If I could be a doctor and work as a medical missionary or any sort of missionary. If I could just teach or preach or (you name it)! If I didn't have this job or did have that one. In other words, although I cannot serve God where I am, I surely could in another place or time.

A friend of mine once worked in an inner-city youth project that sought to bring the gospel to ghetto kids. Once a young man said to him, "You know, I think I really would be a Christian, if I could live in Nashville as you do. But I can't be one here!" One cannot deny that it is easier to live as a Christian in a culture that at least claims Christian values. Yet one is not less acceptable to God where he currently lives. If that were true, we must assume that God can accept ghetto youths only after they have first become middle-class whites. (A first century parallel is the assumption that Gentiles had to become Jewish!)

What we learn in 1 Corinthians 7 is that God accepts people where they are socially, culturally, economically, and geographically. It is the same to God whether one is single or married. All married life is not the same, but one cannot advance his or her acceptability to God by marriage—or its lack. "Each one should remain in the situation" which he was in when God called him" (1 Cor. 7:20, NIV).

Accepting the Call of Others

In the treatment of others Christians also tend to disregard the principle of God's accepting us as we are. Sometimes we have expected (even demanded) others to change their lives socially, culturally, or politically if they really want to be accepted by God (and God's people).

For example, do certain political views make one more acceptable to God than other views? There is a tendency to confuse our political parties with God's favor and to assume dedicated Christians must choose our politics. Must one accept New Deal politics or laissez-faire politics to be a committed Christian? One of my teachers once said of this struggle, "It is not the business of the gospel to make liberals out of conservatives or conservatives out of liberals." I think he saw rightly.

Or what about the matter of one's educational abilities? What about illiterates? Does God equally accept those who can't read or use the King's English properly? Does he hear prayers with *ain'ts* and *uhs*? If one must be fully literate to be a full Christian, then most of the world is already excluded.

To take a more extreme topic, what about the unshaven and the unwashed? In recent years facial hair has become more accepted in the nation, and the church mirrors that acceptance. But 15 years ago bearded men were at least suspect and often not used in the leading of worship. As Americans we tend to share the national prejudice about daily baths, and many really believe the Bible contains the proverb, "Cleanliness is next to godliness."

All these matters relate to 1 Corinthians 7 and the discussion about marriage found there. We claim a mistaken theology when we base our acceptance by God on a changed social situation, whether it is marriage, a job, location, or whatever. God was pleased to accept us as we were when we first heard and believed the gospel. In his book on 1 Corinthians, Hans Conzelmann beautifully summarizes in the statement, "No change of status brought about by myself can advance my salvation."[2] God has already accepted me where he found me.

Although the tradition may be changing somewhat, the Roman Catholic church historically has required those who want to become priests to remain unmarried. This tradition lacks a biblical basis, and most non-Catholics have been very suspicious that an unmarried man could acceptably serve married people. It is somewhat ironic that at the same time other churches have insisted (in practice, if not in theory) that an unmarried man could not serve as a minister! The message of 1 Corinthians 7 specifically denies that one can advance his (or her) station before God by marriage or its absence.

Called to Be

This calling of 1 Corinthians 7 is not to be thought of primarily as God summoning us to a new vocation (secular or religious) as we may think when someone speaks of his occupation as his calling. Rather, calling refers to the situation in which we lived when we heard the gospel and believed it. We should not think of being called as demanding a new occupation (unless we had a sinful occupation) but as giving us new meaning to our old occupation.

In Ephesians 6:5-6, Paul tells slaves to be conscientious in their work, not just to look busy. The reason is that they are "as servants of Christ, doing the will of God." The same point is expressed in 1 Corinthians 7:21f., where slavery is regarded as inconsequential in regard to one's acceptability to God. "For he who was called in the Lord as a slave is a freedman of the Lord. Likewise he who was free when called is a slave of Christ" (7:22). God accepted us on the basis of our faith.

This is not to say that, once called, Christians have no obligations at all to change. Sins should be abandoned and spiritual growth pursued (Eph. 4:28-29). The point is that one should not look at his or her situation in life as needing a different place for spiritual change. We need to abandon that wistful idea that although I can't be a real Christian where I am now, someday or somewhere else I can be. When I have a new job, when we move to a new community, when our kids are grown, when we retire. That is the way one loses life and the purposes and meaning God would give to us now.

Have Faith in God

Ironically, those who insist that they would willingly change their lives in a radical way to serve God are not really showing their willingness to serve him. Rather, they are unable to trust God in the acceptance he has already shown them. The desire to improve our position before God by altering our social situation is a sign of failing faith. Unsure that God can save them, these Christians are trying to save themselves. The Corinthians who were willing to forego marriage or even terminate marriages for their belief in Christ had failed in the most basic way to understand the gospel.

The gospel is not something that fills the small remaining gap between what God demands and the best we can do. The gospel asserts that God accepts men when they respond in trust. God has acted decisively for our salvation. Initially in the sending of Christ and in his saving death and then in the ongoing preaching of that message, God incorporates men and women into the church and gives them privileges to serve where they are.

[1]William Baird, *The Corinthian Church—A Biblical Approach to Urban Culture* (Nashville: Abingdon, 1964). Used by permission.

[2]Conzelmann, *1 Corinthians*, p. 126.

Love and Freedom

7

1 Corinthians 8:1-13; 10:23–11:1

During the Second World War President Franklin Roosevelt delivered a stirring address that has come to be known as the "Four Freedoms" speech. His speech was well in step with the heritage of the United States, for Americans have a tremendous dedication to freedom. Freedom is praised in the U.S. charter documents. The Revolutionary War is also known as "The War for Independence." Americans have often fought wars to seek the freedom of other nations.

Thus it comes as no surprise that freedom is as popular among American Christians as other Americans. Freedom is also an important biblical theme. It is one of the blessings that Christ gives to his people (Gal. 5:1). But because of the way freedom is commonly understood, there is a confusion about Christian freedom. Many Christians believe that freedom means the right to make one's own choices. This type of freedom is praised in such songs as "I've Got to Be Me!" The Greek word for such freedom is *autonomy*, which means "self-ruled."

This passion for freedom has its roots in the Greek democracies. Above all else, Greeks prided themselves upon being free. This concern about individual rights and freedoms is behind the Corinthians' question about food, which Paul discusses in 1 Corinthians 8.

What Shall We Eat?

Of all the ethical questions that occur in 1 Corinthians, perhaps the question concerning meat from sacrificed animals seems the farthest removed from life today. Certainly in America one is most unlikely to encounter the dilemma of whether, as a Christian, he can eat from sacrificed animals. Our meat comes from packing houses, not temples, and, to most people, sacrifice is only a metaphor for refusing a second piece of pie!

To appreciate the seriousness of the question posed to Paul, we must know more about eating habits in first century Corinth. Meat was not a part of the daily diet. Most meals consisted of bread, a thick soup, and, at best, some cheese or fruit. Meat was a highly prized treat.

The Corinthians' question is about "meat sacrificed to idols," referring to the meat taken from the carcass of a slain animal offered to a pagan god. This was the most common source of meat in the diet. Because of the very limited means of preserving meat, the sacrificed meat was eaten or sold immediately. Such meat might be encountered in a variety of ways. It might be bought in a meat market (10:25), many of which were run by temples, or it might be served by a host (10:27). It could be found in one of the meals held in connection with pagan worship (10:19-21) or in a temple dining hall (1 Cor. 8).

The social life of Greek cities revolved around temples. In addition to the regular sacrifices on holy days, many private clubs and trade guilds would hold their meetings in dining rooms and halls owned by pagan temples. Although these monthly meetings were not formally worship gatherings, each would normally include a prayer (and toast!) to the gods. Today a similar pattern is followed by many civic clubs that begin meetings with prayers.

Many people found their social life revolving around such occasional meals. In addition, sacrifices and meals would be associated with the birth of a child, a marriage, entrance into adult life, a job promotion, and death. The meat served at these events, which always included a meal, was first offered in sacrifice. Even radical philosophers who denied the reality of the pagan gods continued to attend such semireligious meals (as today many non-Christians enjoy church socials). Therefore, the question of eating, although obscure today, was very pressing in Paul's day.

The issue was whether one could worship the God of Christians and continue to be involved in civic life, particularly those aspects that had a somewhat religious flavor. According to William Baird, "The temptation to conform to the patterns of the world was an acute problem for the Christians of Corinth. The church there was like a tiny boat tossed about in vast sea of paganism."[1]

Some in Corinth felt that they could participate in this civic life and pursued their beliefs accordingly. Others could not conscientiously participate. The former looked contemptuously on those with "weak consciences," and the latter believed that to follow the example of the strong and eat the meat was to deny Christ.

Knowing and Doing (8:1-8)

An assured truth encountered in most ethical discussions is that one ought to do what he knows is correct. This is so obvious that it seldom occurs to us to question its application. Surely those who know the right ought to do the right. As a general principle, this is correct, but there are cases where it is easily misapplied.

The strong Christians in Corinth argued in their letter for acting according to knowledge. As noted in chapter 6 of this book, Paul often quotes from the Corinthians' letter. In 1 Corinthians 8, he uses quotes regarding idol meat. (In 8:1, 4-5, note the use of quotation marks in many translations, such as the RSV, the NEB, and the NIV.) Although the specific issue of sacrificial meat is not current, many of the arguments used by the Corinthians to defend their decision still are employed today. Therefore, the answers are still important for us.

The Corinthians' first argument is based on knowledge. "All of us possess knowledge" (8:1). They are referring to the knowledge that "an idol has no real existence" and that "there is no God but one" (8:4). They also quoted an early Christian confession that Paul surely knew and may have even taught the Corinthians: "For us there is one God, the Father, from whom are all things and for whom we exist, and one Lord, Jesus Christ, through whom are all things and through whom we exist" (8:6). Objectively, the Corinthians seem to have convincing arguments. Certainly no Christian could deny the truth of their knowledge about the nonbeing of idols! Simply put, their argument is "There are no idols, hence no idol meat!" Accordingly, one may freely eat anything.

The Corinthians' second argument derives from the first—those who have this correct knowledge also have freedom of action. "All things are lawful" (10:23) is probably a Corinthian slogan. The Corinthians argued that to those who understood the Christian faith rightly, there was a full freedom of action. Like most other Greeks—and modern Americans—the Corinthians believed that the greatest good in life is freedom. They regarded Christ as the one who granted freedom to his followers by their special knowledge.

We Were Only Helping (8:9-13)

Although it is possible the "strong" acted with malice toward those they termed "weak," it is equally possible that they acted in good faith. They were only helping the weaker members grow out of their silly fears about the power of idols. They presented arguments the weak could not deny and thus coerced them into following their example. The weaker believers subsequently fell away from Christ after they violated their consciences. No doubt the strong regretted this. However, the stronger believers denied responsibility for the odd quirks of the weaker members. Each Corinthian, especially the less spiritual, expressed his individualism by insisting on his freedom from restraint by others.

In college I became acquainted with two young men who, like myself, came from families that abstained from alcohol. But these students became involved with others who lacked this background and drank very freely. Gradually the two students were encouraged to follow the same habit. However, they could not drink according to their beliefs and soon felt as though they had denied the faith. Their consciences violated, they lost their compass for living and became problem drinkers. Although the conscience is not a completely reliable guide (it is a product of previous training), it is a moral guideline that should not be broken (Rom. 14:23).

Paul emphasizes that the strong are responsible for their effect on the weak. "By your knowledge this weak man is destroyed, the brother for whom Christ died" (8:11). Both the weak and the strong are endangered by the weak's imitation of the strong. In addition, the strong Corinthian believers' plan to "build up" the weak resulted in sinning against the Lord himself (8:12).

Living Responsibly with Others

There are some ethical questions for which the Bible gives clear yes or no answers. Other questions have to be decided case by case. Many churches have experienced tensions and even divisions because leaders have failed to recognize the differences in the two cases.

As far as eating sacrificial meat, there are times when it must be refused, for example, when eating involves obvious worship of idols (10:14-21). At other times it may or may not be permissible, but one answer cannot be given for all situations. The meat itself may be acceptable to eat, for the Lord has provided for our food (10:26). However, the decision whether to eat in a particular situation involves how one lives responsibly with others. Paul gives four guidelines for making such decisions.

Have a proper attitude toward knowledge. Knowledge is a wonderful thing, and we certainly ought to learn as we grow. But knowledge can contribute to wrong decisions in relating to others. First, always following obligations to do what we "know" can become a prison. For example, many doctors have trouble understanding abortion as an ethical problem; they view it as a technical one. By thinking this way, the knowledge of the means becomes justification for the act.

Paul seems to agree that the pagan gods are not real and thus that food sacrificed to them has not been harmed. Nevertheless, this knowledge does not require one to eat if others are endangered by his eating. The Christian is freed from his knowledge so that he does not have to employ it at each opportunity.

Second, knowledge, as understood at Corinth, is not the primary way Christians should relate to God. Remember that 1 Corinthians 1 stressed that human knowledge is not the path to God. In 8:2-3 Paul says that our knowledge may not be as impressive as we often suppose it to be. What counts is not that *we know* something about God but that *God knows* us and recognizes us as his servants. God's work—not our knowing God—is first in salvation.

Have a proper attitude toward freedom. In the mid and late sixties, American college campuses were filled with chants of "freedom now." This belief was expressed in dress, hairstyles, "streaking," and more illegal demonstrations. To many it seemed obvious that the highest possible good was personal freedom. The same evaluation of individual freedom was held by the Corinthians and is widely held by many Christians today, especially in making decisions about personal conduct. The essence of this individualistic freedom was captured in Paul's day by the philosopher Epictetus who said, "He is free who does as he wills." In our time it is best summed up in the song, "I Did It My Way."

Paul too was a proponent of Christian freedom. Perhaps the Corinthians regarded his preaching of freedom from sin, death, and the law as a Christian endorsement of the Greek passion for individual freedom. However, Paul had a different understanding of a Christian's freedom than the Corinthians did.

First, Paul did not see freedom as the greatest good to which all other goods must be subjected. Second, he did not see freedom as the right to do as one pleases, but as the opportunity and power to do as God desires.

When one understands freedom as a personal right, he always asks when making decisions, "How am I benefited or injured?" This was the approach the Corinthians used in eating sacrificial meat. But the gospel teaches that the greatest good is to act in consideration of the brother and how he is benefited or injured. Thus one should not simply consider whether he feels right about eating but how his brother feels (8:9-13). Paul summarizes this approach in 10:33, "I try to please all men in everything I do, not seeking my own advantage, but that of many." This course of action imitates Jesus (11:1), who counted the benefit of others rather than himself (Phil. 2:5-11).

A very helpful discussion of freedom is found in Galatians 5:13-14. Here the call of God is to freedom. But Paul warns that freedom can also become an opportunity (literally "beachhead") for the flesh. The liberating work of God can be perverted into worldliness. The devil is never disarmed, for he can use God's own gifts to entrap believers.

To keep freedom from again becoming bondage to fleshly desires, Paul admonishes the Galatians to "be servants of one another" through love. Therefore, to use freedom rightly is to serve one another. "For the whole law is fulfilled in one word, 'you shall love your neighbor as yourself'" (Gal. 5:14).

Pursue humble results. As Christians, we can know if our freedom and knowledge are being used rightly by the result of our actions.

The Corinthians' exercise of their freedom led to excessive pride and jealousy in the church. Paul graphically terms this result as "puffed up" (8:1). He depicts a person who actually is small but inflated like a balloon to unreasonable size by his self-estimate (one might say "filled with hot air").

Use freedom and knowledge to build up. The alternative to "puffed up" is "built up." Older translations render 1 Corinthians 8:1 as "love edifies," a perfectly acceptable translation as long as we recall that the word "edify" originally referred to construction work (an *edifice* is a building). Apparently this word was taken from the proud Corinthians, who regarded their brave example as a way to "edify" the weaker members to eat (8:10). Like most modern people, they understood "edification" as the individual enlarging his faith.

The correct use of knowledge and freedom leads to the building up of the whole body of Christ, which is God's temple (3:16). In making edification the test of our conduct, it is vital to realize that this does not mean advancing our own spirituality but the growth of the community of faith. One does not edify himself, nor even another person, but the whole church is "built up" (Eph. 2:19-22).

So Who's Right?

In most conflicts on ethical issues, the arbitrator is asked, "Who is right?" The strong Corinthians wrote the apostle Paul to argue their case based on a supposed correct understanding of doctrine, and confident Paul shared with them a high value on freedom. Did Paul take their side or that of the weak? The answer is neither.

It is interesting to contrast Paul's approach in this matter with that of the Corinthians. Paul does not have a program for convincing the weak believers of the Christian's freedom to eat sacrificial meat, although elsewhere he agrees such meat is not unclean (Rom. 14:6, 14). He accepts the weak man as a brother for whom Christ died and has no compulsion to change him.

This whole discussion has often been interpreted to say that Paul agreed with the strong in theory but insisted on giving up one's freedom in practice out of consideration for the weak brother. This interpretation sets in contrast freedom and love; one must at times constrain his freedom of action out of love for others.

Church relationships would gain much if this approach could be followed, but it is still short of what we are being taught here. It still defines freedom as egocentric. Paul's approach is more radical. Love is an *act*, not a restriction, of freedom. The person in Christ, claimed by God for his kingdom of grace, for the first time is really free from his self-centeredness to love others. Because we have understood the true character of Christ's love for us, we have the freedom *not* to exercise our knowledge. We need not prove that we are free to anyone, to the weaker brother, to Christ, or even to ourselves. By accepting God's freedom, we can give up the need to prove it.

When we act to benefit others (10:24), we are not restricting our freedom. We are exercising it in love.

[1] Baird, *The Corinthian Church—A Biblical Approach To Urban Culture*, p. 89.

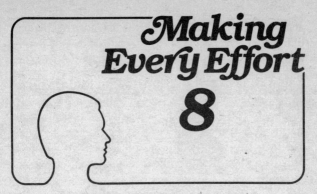

Making Every Effort

8

1 Corinthians 9:1-27; 10:1-13

Many people understand love to be opposite duty and obligation. One may either act from demand or from love. This dichotomy derives partly from the belief that genuine love must be spontaneous, arising in an unexpected moment (like the popular idea of "falling in love"). Although the content and contours of Christian love are more fully examined in chapter 11, the relationship of love to duty and effort will be explored in this chapter.

Meeting Love's Demands

In 1 Corinthians 8 Paul argues that Christians must consider the effects of their actions on others, even when the actions appear not to be sinful. But he apparently suspects that some may object to being held responsible for how other Christians react. Those who wanted to eat sacrificial meat disregarded the effects of this eating on others and insisted on their rights.

Thus in 1 Corinthians 9 Paul applies the principle of responsible love to himself. He makes clear that neither love nor responsibility comes easily; both require effort. The effort demanded for Christian love contrasts with the popular bumper sticker slogan, "Let Go and Let God."

The slogan implies that genuine love and service are achieved without work.

A Certain Right Rejected (9:1-18)

First Corinthians 9 is really an oddity. Paul appears to be very defensive about his apostleship as he begins this chapter. In verses 1 and 2 he argues that he is as much an apostle as the others, especially to the Corinthians, who owe their Christian faith to his preaching. They cannot deny Paul's apostleship without denying their foundation of belief!

Then in verses 3-15 Paul argues very strongly for his right to be financially supported by the Corinthians. In support of this right, he presents as examples the conduct of the other apostles (9:5-6), military and farm living (9:7), scripture from the Old Testament (9:8-10, citing Deut. 25:4), the Corinthians' support of others (9:11-12), the priests at the temple (9:13), and even the word of the Lord (9:14). He clearly makes a long, comprehensive argument.

After this tedious argument, Paul surprisingly states, "But I have made no use of any of these rights, nor am I writing this to secure any such provision" (9:15). In the same verse he says, "I would rather die" than to do so. A very strong conflict seems to exist between Paul's belief and his practice. Why does Paul strongly argue for his rights, only to reject them once he established his case? Paul is using his own situation to illustrate the theme of 1 Corinthians 9—love demanding effort—which is better expressed in 9:19-23.

Serving and Standing Firm (9:19-23)

. Paul rather boldly describes how he adapted his conduct before different groups. Because today Paul is highly regarded—though seldom imitated—we have difficulty realizing that when he penned these letters, his authority was not quickly granted by churches in all matters. His letters were part of an ongoing dialogue between him and his converts in which the outcome was not certain and Paul's position was often debated. In this period some criticized Paul for being less than consistent and modifying his plans and positions rather easily.

Was Paul in fact an opportunist? Does he confess as much in 1 Corinthians 9? He says he was as a Jew among Jews and as one without the law (that is, a Gentile) to those without the law. Passages from other letters reveal that some criticized him from two opposite positions.

The Charges

In other letters Paul is very defensive about his relationship with the church in Jerusalem. In Galatians 1:10-11 he defends himself against the charge that he conducts his work to win the approval of men (notice that the charge is "*still* pleasing men"). Apparently the Galatians had been led to believe that Paul told them less than the full gospel and that in other places he was "still preaching circumcision" (Gal. 5:11). Those people who caused him trouble accused him of dishonesty, claiming he did not keep the law in Galatia but did elsewhere. No doubt some Gentile Christians felt Paul was too bound to the outdated traditions of Judaism.

In Romans 3:8 Paul faces accusations from the opposite quarter. He cites a rumor circulated about him: "Why not say—as we are being slanderously reported as saying and as some claim that we say—let us do evil that good may result" (JB). This time his critics say Paul is removing the boundaries necessary to maintain Christian conduct and, by preaching grace, tempting men to sin. They would have recognized—and criticized—his claim to be as one without the law to those outside the law.

Thus Paul has the dubious achievement of having alienated both the more conservative Jewish Christians and the more liberal Gentile ones. He was regarded as too traditional by some and as too bent toward grace only by others. Perhaps when these two groups in Corinth compared impressions, the charge arose that Paul was as uncertain as his travel plans, saying yes and no in the same breath (2 Cor. 1:15-20). This sort of charge was made possible by his adaptive policy as stated in 1 Corinthians 9:19-23.

Some Evidence of Paul's Method

Another source of possible criticism of Paul's vacillations is 1 Corinthians 8, where Paul's practice differs from his theoretical views. In chapter 8 Paul agrees with those in Corinth who quote the correct doctrinal formulation, "For us there is one God, the Father, from whom all things come and for whom we exist, and one Lord, Jesus Christ, through whom are all things and through whom we exist" (8:6). Accordingly, the Corinthians are correct in claiming, "An idol has no real existence," and "there is no God but the one" (8:4). Because there are no idols, it follows that there can be no idol meat! In all this Paul agrees. However, he concludes 1 Corinthians 8 by offering to renounce any and all meat if opportunity demands it (8:13).

Still another example of Paul's apparent ambivalence is in 1 Corinthians 7. This chapter considers whether marriage is best for Christians. Again Paul quotes approvingly the Corinthians' slogan, "It is well for a man not to touch a woman" (7:1), and he wishes that all were single as he is (7:7). However, in this same chapter he strongly defends marriage and insists that any marriage must be genuine (including the sexual aspect suspect to the Corinthians). He also supports the unmarried in decisions to marry or not. Clearly his position seems unclear.

All Things to Everybody

Does it then turn out that Paul was only a religious weathercock, shifting his position according to the breeze? Such an interpretation of Paul is very hard to accept, partly because we believe that telling others where we stand is the most approved course for Christians. Many people don't worry about how others feel about them; they just "let the chips fall where they may." Thus we are critical of any view that makes Paul appear wishy-washy.

It is true that Paul had his faults too, and perhaps one of them was inconsistency. However, before we attribute to some failure his policy of adapting to his audience, we ought to consider the reason Paul himself gives for his wavering behavior.

In Paul's explanation of his life as an apostle, including his accepting support from some churches and refusing it from others, Paul insists that he is guided by principle. "I have become all things to all men, that I might by all means save some" (9:22). This principle applies not only when he introduces the gospel to men but as he lives with others in Christ (remember the specific issue is accepting support from the Corinthians).

How seriously do we take Paul's instruction to do everything to save some? Apparently we are willing to accept and be rather charitable about bad habits, faults, and sins of outsiders whom we are seeking to win to Christ. We will overlook these sins in order "to save some." However, such strenuous effort of accepting and dealing lovingly with others is also necessary for many Christians "to save some." In being charitable of the imperfections and sins of others as they seek to improve, we must not overlook other Christians (Gal. 6:1, 10).

It is this intention to be a man for others and to accept the hard demands it makes that Paul says is decisive in all his work. Rather than seeking to improve his reputation or following, Paul seeks to benefit others—Jew, Greek, strong, weak—to improve their commitments. Therefore, he is not really without law (or principle), as some may suspect (9:20), but rather is under an altogether new law. This principle is not designed to increase one's own status but to aid others.

The Law of Christ (9:21)

Paul says that he is under the "law of Christ" (9:21). This expression has been often understood as being under the New Testament instead of the law of Moses. However, this solution is doubtful, because when Paul penned these lines, there was no New Testament.

Instead, the expression "law of Christ" is to be understood in terms of the parallel usage in Galatians 6:2: "Bear one another's burdens, and so fulfil the law of Christ." Stated positively, the "law of Christ" is selfless ministry to others. This is what Paul meant in 1 Corinthians 9 when he said he became as a Jew to Jews, as a Gentile to Gentiles, and as weak to the weak.

Additional insight on the meaning of the "law of Christ" is found in the verses preceding Galatians 6:2. In 5:25-26 Paul urges Christians to live by the Spirit, not the flesh. How does one do this? "Let us have no self-conceit, no provoking of one another, no envy of one another" (5:26). This admonition fits exactly with the situation in Corinth. Some believers were conceited about their gifts (1 Cor. 12) and their wisdom (1 Cor. 2). Others were envious of some they believed more mature and more spiritual than themselves. In regard to the many ethical problems we have already studied, it is clear some Christians provoked other believers. In each of these ways, the Corinthians failed to follow the law of Christ.

The law of Christ is related to the Great Commandment, which is frequently found in the New Testament. In Galatians 5:13-15, the obligations Christians have to each other are set forth. Here we are reminded of Jesus' own words. "The whole law is fulfilled in one word, 'You shall love your neighbor as yourself'" (Gal. 5:14). Whether or not Paul actually means by "law of Christ" the response Jesus gave when asked about the greatest commandment, Paul and Jesus are saying the same thing—consideration of others should come before oneself.

From this examination of Galatians, we can better understand what Paul means by the law of Christ, and we can see that Paul is not really the lawless renegade some strict Christians suspected. Nor is he the unbending legalist some freedom-loving Christians feared. Paul recommends a course of Christian conduct that is not at all "unprincipled." Rather, it is modeled upon a principle unparalleled in a world of competition, selfishness, and envy.

Paul is following the example of Jesus, who also did not consider his interests but became a servant of others (Phil. 2:5-11).

When we have differences with others, we often choose to confront the others. But Paul teaches us to accommodate ourselves to the needs of others as much as possible. Of course, Paul is not advocating wrong doing. He is saying that we may have to do what we do not personally favor or like. This is a way of accepting others for their good.

It Ain't Easy (9:24-27)

There is a predictable response whenever this principle of modifying one's life for the advantage of others is set forth. "That is just taking the easy way out!" Adapting to the needs and expectations of others, rather than asserting one's views, is often regarded as cowardice.

Looking again at 1 Corinthians 9, Paul concludes that adapting his life to the expectations and needs of others is not that easy. Using metaphors taken from athletics, he compares this with the effort required to win a footrace or participate in a boxing match (9:24-27). (Corinth was the site of the second largest games in Greece, so these analogies are well chosen.) This sort of effort is required to follow a course of putting others' interests ahead of our own.

My experiences have confirmed the truth of this assertion. Defending the correctness of my views and the reasonableness of my actions is much easier than allowing others to have their differing opinions or permitting them to disagree with my own. This is partly because of the great power of human pride and partly because we prefer to be "right" right now. So we settle for our verdict of justification rather than having to wait for God's. Here again is the observation that love is not easy; it is very demanding. It requires a lot of effort not to insist on our way.

Consider Israel's Struggle (10:1-13)

Because the Corinthians were so confident in their Christian life, they believed that no effort was required to maintain a good relationship with God. For this reason they lacked self-discipline, especially in foregoing their rights to benefit others.

In addition to his personal example of putting others first (9:19-23), Paul also cites the example of Israel. These people of God had also enjoyed his saving hand and his guiding presence in their journey. Yet they were rejected for their sins. Despite great advantages God's elect can forfeit their salvation.

In recounting the exodus (10:1-5), Paul stresses how everyone (note "all" occurs five times) had passed through the sea (analogous to the baptism of Christians) and shared the divinely provided meals (parallel to the Lord's Supper). Yet "with *most* of them God was not pleased."

Some of the specific sins that evoked God's punishment are given in 10:6-10, but the general point is summarized in verse 12, "Therefore let anyone who thinks that he stands take heed lest he fall." The Corinthians, like many Christians after them, became overconfident and ceased striving for the rest, not because God cannot be counted upon (10:13), but because Christians fail to persevere.

There are many ways in which Christians may lose their salvation by lack of diligence. Among these is the failure to make every effort to work for the spiritual life of others. In striving to be acceptable to God, we must also strive to be accepting of others.

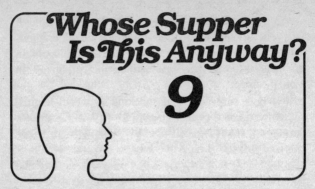

Whose Supper Is This Anyway?

9

1 Corinthians 10:14-22; 11:17-34

One of the most enriching and pleasant aspects of family holiday gatherings is the meal shared together. There family members who have not seen each other for a long time—sometimes many years—renew their common love around a common table. The ability of a shared meal to create and express common interests and commitments is also recognized in the Bible. For example, in Luke 15:22-24 the joyous reunion of the prodigal's family was manifested in the feast. In Acts 2:42, one of the marks of the early church was its sharing of table fellowship. In fact, the blessing of heaven is illustrated in the sharing of a feast (Luke 22:28-30; Rev. 19:9). The present anticipation of that heavenly meal is the Lord's Supper. However, this communion was a problem in Corinth.

What Was Going On? (11:17-22)

Once again, before we can properly understand what Paul is teaching about the Supper, we must reconstruct the other side of the conversation. What was happening in Corinth that led Paul to correct the practice there?

Although the Lord's Supper was mentioned in connection with the discussion of sacrificial meat (see chapter 8 of this book), the most direct treatment of the communion in Corinth is in 11:17-34. From the criticisms in these verses, we can reconstruct the problems in Corinth.

It is both surprising and shocking that Paul begins, "When you come together it is not for the better but for the worse" (11:17). Perhaps many believe that any observance of the Supper—certainly if it is done sincerely—is better than none. What could be so bad that Paul would think it best not even to meet?

The Corinthians erred by being divisive when assembling as a church. The Corinthian tendency to form cliques has already been discussed. Nevertheless, this division at the table of the Lord was so serious that Paul concludes "it is not the Lord's Supper that you eat" (11:20). Why not? Surely the Corinthians thought they were eating the Lord's Supper. They had not met to worship some pagan deity. Yet the *manner* in which they observed the communion was so foreign to its intent, it could not be properly called the Lord's Supper. It was not the *Lord's* Supper because they did not consider the church as the body of the Lord when partaking. "Each one" (11:21) had his own meal.

In addition to communion, the Corinthian church probably had a fuller meal—the "love feast" (Jude 12; 2 Pet. 2:13; Acts 2:42, 46). Such meals were a common feature of both Greek and Jewish religious groups. Jesus' own practice of eating with his disciples is similar. Whether the Corinthians had separated the communion from the meal in a clearcut manner or had united them is unknown. That they had a full meal is implicit in the rebuke that some overindulged (11:21).

Basically, there are four specific charges about the Corinthian misuse of this meal.

91

They did not wait for some. If someone is going to be late for a dinner engagement, he or she often calls the host and says, "Please start without me." Usually the host will insist upon waiting. Clearly, consideration of others is important in beginning a meal.

Apparently in Corinth some who arrived early began the meal instead of waiting for the other members. This practice—an expression of Corinthian individualism—created the divisions at the table.

Interestingly, meals in Greek religious associations were held in a similar manner. These meals lasted several hours, and, although some food was provided (usually the meat), individual members also brought some items, much like today's covered dish dinners. The participants would feel free to eat the food they brought without waiting for others. In addition, the fact that the early church met in private houses clarifies why the Corinthians would regard eating times as a matter for the host to determine.

Some did not receive. Some were being left out of the meal, either because they could not afford to bring anything to eat or because they arrived too late. Some—perhaps slaves who had to wait until their owner did not need their services—worked late into the evening and could not arrive in time to eat. Others—perhaps those with a more ample financial situation—could control their schedules and arrive early with enough food.

The poor are embarrassed. In verse 22 Paul puts in perspective the motives of this premature, private taking of the church meal. Only two possible explanations are considered. Either those who ate early are despising the "have nots," or they have no other place to eat. Obviously the first motive is the true one.

This humiliation of poorer members is not only an offense to them but is also an attack on the church of God.

When Christians fail to include—either on purpose or by carelessness—some members in fellowship meals and other gatherings, this is not merely a social error but a religious affront. Even if the event is a simple church supper, Christians need consciously to encourage members to participate—even those who may only be able to bring a loaf of bread or an appetite!

Some overindulge and become drunk. In view of the Greek passion for wine, this probably happened. Many descriptions of Greek religious meals stress the joy of drink and the fines assessed to those whose joy gets out of hand. The recently converted Corinthians may not have given up their past habits (6:10-11 includes drunkards). Or this description might be a dramatic overstatement of the disparity between those who do have a share of the meal and others who have no part.

This disturbance in Corinth seems far removed from present day because churches do not have a full meal in the worship service that could be abused. However, there are still important lessons for us in this discussion. It is a reminder that our manner of treating others, especially when we claim to act in Jesus' name, can render our worship acceptable. Jesus makes this point in Matthew 25:31-45. As James Thompson says, "One may take the Lord's Supper with total seriousness; he may be faithful in his participation. But if he neglects his brother and forgets the rest of the community it is not the Lord's Supper at all." [1]

Communion and Fellowship (10:14-22)

The Greek word translated "communion" in 10:16-17 is *koinonia*, one of those few terms that have become somewhat familiar to non-Greek readers. *Communion* is the equivalent Latin word. When someone speaks of the "communion," what subconscious definition do we have?

93

Communion and individualism. Several years ago I toured a college in Wisconsin that trains priests for the Roman Catholic church. In the basement of a building were several small cubicles about the size of a pantry, which each student was assigned for his private worship. Among other things, each room contained bread and wine for a private communion, called "mass" by Catholics.

At the time it struck me how far removed that was from what we are taught in 1 Corinthians. Since then, however, I have wondered how different their understanding was from our own. Although we do not have brick partitions, many Christians would like to seal off the outside world, including other worshippers. The desired goal of private devotion with God may be similar. Think of the extreme individualism of many communion hymns, which speak of a private relationship between the individual and God in the communion.

Fellowship in the Body. "Communion" is best understood by noting what word it translates. *Koinonia* literally means "that which we have in common." Its frequent occurrences in the New Testament are also translated: "fellowship" (Acts 2:42; 1 Cor. 1:9), "taking part" (2 Cor. 8:3), and even "contribution" (Rom. 15:26; 2 Cor. 9:13). All these translations stress the belief that Christians have a shared relationship because of their joint life in Christ. That relationship is what the communion is.

Understandably, Christians use this biblical idea to speak of church socials as "fellowship." However, fellowship should be extended to include the Lord's Supper (and the contribution!). Christians have fellowship in the Supper through the special relationship enjoyed with Christ and with other Christians. The Corinthians failed to consider an awareness of this mutual relationship in their observance of the Lord's Supper. "Every time the church forgets that the Lord's Supper is a fellowship, it agrees more with Paul's opponents than with Paul himself."[2]

Shared Perspectives (11:23-26)

A favorite device that storytellers like to use is the idea of a time machine. Any parent with children who watch the Saturday morning cartoons can attest to this! Returning to Chapter 11, we see that in some ways the Lord's Supper is like a time machine, because it presents differing temporal angles of our mutual life.

Our shared history. First the Lord's Supper looks backward to its institution by Jesus. The communion is rooted in the last supper, which Jesus shared with his disciples as he taught them of the New Covenant. Perhaps Paul refers to this event here to remind the "super spiritual" Corinthians, who neglected daily living as Christians, that their Lord died.

The Lord's Supper is also a memorial. Unfortunately, the word memorial is commonly associated with tombstones (cemeteries are frequently called "memorial parks") and gifts given in memory of departed friends. For some, this association turns the Lord's Supper into a funeral meal. But the communion does not speak of a departed friend; it commemorates a present Lord who joins us at his table. You don't hold a wake for someone who is alive!

The memorial part of the communion connects those who share the Lord's Supper with the establishment of a New Covenant by the death of Jesus (11:23-25). This activity reminds us of that convenant in the way that Israel was reminded of the decisive events in her relationship with God by certain repeated ceremonies (Exod. 13:3-10; Num. 10:10). By remembering the last meal in which Jesus established the New Convenant, Christians claim Jesus' death "for us."

Our shared present. The Lord's Supper is not only a word about our past; it is also about the present life. Paul says that in eating and drinking the cup we preach (proclaim) the death of the Lord. When Christians repeat the meal that establishes the New Israel, we remind ourselves and teach those who witness it that Jesus' death has a present meaning. If God is seen in Christ, Christ is revealed today in the Lord's Supper.

This proclamation may call upon Christians to retell the story of our salvation when partaking the Supper. This would parallel the practice of the Jewish Passover in which part of the ceremony told the whole history of Israel to teach the meaning of the meal. Or it may be that the eating itself is a symbolic way (such as the dusting off of one's shoes) to make known the death of the Lord.

Our shared hope. If there is any aspect of the communion more under-emphasized today than fellowship, it is probably the Lord's return. The teaching on the last day is generally neglected. The Corinthians believed that they had already reached the highest level of spirituality possible, thus eliminating the need for a resurrection (see chapter 13 of the book).

The prospective angle of the Lord's Supper is expressed in one phrase—"until he comes." The prayer of 16:22—"Our Lord, come!"—shows the lively expectation in the early church (see Luke 13:27-35; 22:29-30; Rev. 3:20). Because the Lord's Supper is a time of deep realization of the Lord's first coming, it is reasonable to conclude that it also points to his return.

The Danger of the Supper (11:27-34)

Few people really enjoy grammar. Some will recall being asked to "diagram" a sentence to clarify its grammatical structure. However, if more attention had been paid to the grammar of the King James' translation of 1

Corinthians 11:27, many Christians would have been spared a harmful misunderstanding that is rather widely held.

Some people have declined to participate in the Lord's Supper at times because they didn't feel worthy. Of course, who really could feel worthy of the Lord's sacrifice? After all, Jesus died to save *sinners*, not angels. However, in verse 27 "unworthy" is an *adverb*, not an *adjective*. Thus it refers not to the person who partakes but to the manner in which the Supper is observed.

Discern the body. How were the Corinthians partaking "in an unworthy manner"? Clearly, they neglected those members who had little to share in the church meal and whose circumstances forced them to arrive late. This is explicitly stated earlier. But how is this criticism related to the one "who eats and drinks without discerning the body" and to self-examination (11:28-31)? What does *body* mean here?

Looking ahead to 1 Corinthians 12, it seems best to regard *body* here as a reference to the body of Christ assembled at table—the church (12:12). The church is Christ's body in the world today (1 Cor. 12:27; Eph. 1:23; 4:12; Col. 1:18; 3:15). Of course, the members of Christ's church are the body, whether or not they are assembled for worship. But in sharing that common meal Christians are most visibly Christ's body.

This means that failure to discern the body is the same as disregarding some members when sharing the communion. Failing to recognize the mutual bonds among the members of the body and neglecting some believers is overlooking the body that the Lord has now.

This problem may not seem like a present danger, but in at least two ways these instructions apply to Christians today.

First, does the manner of partaking help one to understand what the Lord's Supper is? Is the Supper seen as a way to realize the death of the Lord and the presence of the New Covenant? Is this explained so that member and visitor alike are instructed? Is the community character—the "fellowship" of the communion—appreciated, or is the Supper considered a private matter between each individual and his Lord?

Second, our ideas and concepts do affect our actions. The Corinthians' mistaken, individualized view of the Lord's Supper has harmful consequences today. It results in treating the communion too personally, neglecting participation with the whole church. Usually some members arrive late, but they are still in time for the communion. Others hurry out after the Supper. These have little interest in the singing, the sermon, or the giving. Those who would criticize should first consider that these people are only acting out the logical consequences of the teaching about the Lord's Supper.

Examine himself. The call for self-examination in 11:28 is widely regarded as a personal review of one's spiritual condition. Except when it prevents one from taking action (the "paralysis of analysis"), self-examination, at any time, including the Lord's Supper is a good practice.

However, it is probable that something more specific is meant here. After Paul's rebuke of the Corinthians' neglecting their brethren in the common assembly, verse 28 is most likely a warning to each member to consider his own conduct in this regard. Does each consider the whole body of Christ when sharing the Lord's Supper? When hosting the common meal? Or does each neglect some and embarrass them in that which was intended to be a time of Christian fellowship? This point seems clear in the summarizing admonition of 11:33-34: "When you come together to eat, wait for one another . . . lest you . . . be condemned."

Because the work of Christ is to reconcile men to God and to each other, it is inappropriate if one's worship becomes a means of dividing brethren. After all, it is the *Lord's* Supper to which everyone is an invited guest.

---

[1] Thompson, *Our Life Together*, p. 70.
[2] Thompson, p. 74.

Belonging through Diversity

10

1 Corinthians 12:1-31

One can go into almost any bookstore or supermarket in the nation and find biographies which tell how a person was "born again." Of course, these books are usually about famous people in entertainment, sports or politics (there seems to be less interest in a more common person's rebirth).

What is frequently common to these various accounts is that they see Christianity as very private and individualistic. There are very few good words for organized religion, and the basic theme is the individual's finding God. This same individualism was also found in first-century Corinth.

Influenced by the individualism of their culture, some of the Corinthian Christians were using their spiritual gifts to prove that they were spiritually superior to their fellow Christians. In 1 Corinthians 12 Paul corrects this self-centeredness by saying that they are the body of Christ. Each part works for the common good, not for self-enhancement. Whenever the unity of the church is threatened by individualism, the underlying message of 1 Corinthians 12 applies: diverse spiritual abilities enable unity of the body, not spiritual competition among the members.

The Mark of the Spirit (12:1-3)

Almost any interview with a member or a coach of a football team will mention "team spirit." A recent win will be attributed to the players' spirit or, conversely, a loss to their lack of spirit. We may even refer to someone who is very excited about his belief or work by saying, "He's got the spirit!" This use of "spirit" to convey deeply felt excitement is very close to a common feature of Greek religion.

The New Testament, and especially Paul's writings, makes clear that the Spirit is an integral part of Christian life. From the first days of the church, the Spirit was understood to be given to those who accepted the preaching of Jesus as the Christ (Acts 2:38; 5:32). Paul and the Corinthians share a deep belief in the Spirit as the mark of a Christian (1 Cor. 3:16; 6:19). However, as he turns to the topic of spiritual gifts, Paul reminds the Corinthians that their own pagan past should prove that a "spiritual experience" is not always reliable.

A deeply felt attachment to a god was part of the pagan religions (12:2) which the Corinthians had left. There too they had "felt irresistibly drawn" (12:2 JB) by the idols. Thus it is obvious that one cannot rely upon an excited feeling to determine whether God approves our conduct.

It is possible that some Corinthians felt they were led by the Spirit to say a curse upon Jesus (12:3), but more probably Paul uses this very strong contrast to show that not every action can be sanctioned just because Christians have the Spirit. However, on the other hand, the simplest and most basic act of faith ultimately comes from God's Spirit when we confess: "Jesus is Lord" (12:3, cf. Rom. 8:14-17; 10:9; John 16:13, 14 and Gal. 4:6).

At the very start of this discussion Paul gives two principles which will guide what follows in chapter 12 and also in chapter 14. First, the Spirit does indwell and empower Christians, all Christians. Second, even when the Spirit is working through us we remain subject to evaluation and correction by other members (1 Cor. 14:32, 37; 1 John 4:1). This means no one can claim immunity from instruction or discipline on the basis of having the Spirit.

These are important points today as well. We also encounter some who insist that because they are "spiritual" people their deeds and claims ought not to be tested by others. Reacting to that, others deny the work of the Spirit in any way today, lest the claims of such "spirit filled" people be acknowledged as true. However, both approaches are wrong.

If one is led to confess Jesus as Lord, not only in words but also in deed, then the first criteria of being led by God's Spirit is met. That is basic. However, if this does not happen, then it is not *God's* Spirit, although it still may be *a* spirit.

One Spirit, Diverse Gifts (12:4-11)

America has long prided itself on being an international "melting pot" of peoples and cultures. This multinational heritage gives a very different weave to our society than that found in most countries. But this diversity has always created a tension between holding to our diverse heritages and remaining one nation.

In 1 Corinthians 12:4-11 there is a discussion about unity and diversity in the Corinthian church regarding spiritual gifts. Chapter 12 and chapter 14 clearly show that the Corinthians were troubled by the tendency of some to stress the gift of tongues above all other gifts. The first reply Paul gives to this troublesome tendency is to insist on the diversity of spiritual gifts.

Paul enumerates nine spiritual gifts (12:8-10) which do not exhaust such gifts, but are only representative. His point is that there is a variety of such gifts, all given by the one Spirit (12:4, 11). No one gift is heralded as more valuable than another, for all forms of Christian work come from the same God, Lord and Spirit (12:4-6).

Concerning the diversity of gifts. Two points are crucial. First, no Christian should feel less significant than another because of his or her gift, just as no Christian ought to feel superior to others. The same God inspires these gifts, "all in every one" (12:6). It is the one Spirit who apportions them as he wishes (12:11). Second, these gifts are not given for the benefit of their recipients but are "for the common good" (12:7). The diversity is to complement each other.

One Spirit, One Body (12:12, 13)

There is the closest of relationships between a person and his body. In fact, the body is the "self." This intimate relationship is of great importance for understanding 1 Corinthians 12:12, 13.

Perhaps you have heard sermons point out that Christ has no hands but our hands, and no tongue but our tongue. Usually this thought is to spur us to greater efforts in service and mission. And, in a fundamental way, it is true. Yet we ought to avoid the impression that Christ is powerless to affect the world unless we do it for him. Rather, the point is that Christ does affect the world, and through Christians. This is the point of the description of the church as the body of Christ.

The equating of the church and the body was encountered earlier in 1 Corinthians 10. In both passages the actual message is not that the church is like Christ's body, but that it *is* Christ's body (the "with" in the RSV

103

translation of 12:12 is without textual warrant). Christ and his followers are one person. One is baptized into Christ because he is baptized into the church which is Christ's body.

Paul continues in verses 14-26 to employ this body image as a metaphor by speaking of the unity and diversity of the human body. Yet the church as a body is not just similar to any body one may think of, it is *Christ's* body—the body of a particular person.

Many Christians have tried to pattern their lives after the picture of Jesus in the gospels, both out of a respect for the Savior and a realization that his words have abiding value. These characteristics of Jesus are widely regarded as valuable for individuals, but often their relevance for the life of the whole church is overlooked. As the body of Christ, the church also ought to adopt the attitudes and values, conduct and spirit which Jesus presents in the gospels. The present body of Christ should resemble the first body of Christ.

To take just one example, it is clear that in the gospels although Jesus associated with a wide spectrum of peoples, primarily his ministry was to those who lacked much of the world's goods. Yet very often when churches consider programs or location, we seek to impress those of greater incomes. Perhaps churches have looked for those who could serve us, rather than those we might serve.

One Body Through Diversity (12:14-26)

The expression often heard around election time, "the body politic" can actually be traced back to five centuries before Christ to the Greek democracies which spoke of the city by analogy to the human body. A Roman general, using "body" as a metaphor for the city, once convinced rebellious slaves that their work stoppage was hurting them as much as the wealthy of the city. Thus a metaphorical use of "body" is well-known before Paul.

The metaphorical use of body here is to convince the seemingly less spectacular members of the value of their (seemingly less impressive) gifts. The argument is that no *one* member is the body, just as no one part of the human body is the body. The human body is made up of a variety of members, and it is precisely the variety which makes it a body. How ridiculous it would be to have a body which was all eye or all ear. That would not be a body, but a medical curiosity to be placed in a bottle in a laboratory. The body *is* the working together of the various members.

This analogy has implications both for those who feel that their part is not so important (vss. 14-18) and for those who feel they are more important (vss. 19-26). Those who think they are less valuable need to recall that it is God who arranged the body (vs. 18), and he determined the variety of parts which are necessary. No part of the human body can be withdrawn without injury to the whole, nor can a member of Christ's body.

This means no Christian can regard some members as only "excess baggage" who are not really necessary (vss. 14, 21). In the human body some more sensitive, although less powerful, parts are actually treated with higher regard (vss. 22, 23), and this also God has done with the body of Christ (vs. 24). Paul attacks the extreme individualism of the Corinthians who are too arrogant and those who are too insecure in their self-estimate.

Perennial problems. These attitudes among various members of the body of Christ are as common today as they were when Paul wrote the chapter. If we were to analyze most congregations, we would find a small "core" group who actually does most of the ministry and receives most of the honors. We would also find another, outer group who receives little or no recognition and appears to be very unproductive.

There is a temptation for both groups to imitate the Corinthians in their analysis of each group's worth to God and to others. The very active may regard the inactive as "hangers on" who are spiritual parasites. The less active may consider themselves second-class citizens in the kingdom of God and resent the critical judgment of others.

Seeking solutions. The body metaphor offers some directions in working with these tensions. First, those in leadership roles need to stress the value of all members. Few people will live up to any more than others expect of them. We need to take seriously the church as the body of Christ. It is not just an organization which we direct and administer; it belongs to Christ. This alone assures each and every member of his importance to God.

The body imagery also implies that each member has a stake in all other members. Like the Corinthians we are tempted by our culture's individualism to think that we are responsible only for our own achievements and failures. That is an "eye-only" view of the body. If we learn to "have the same care for one another," then the "discord in the body" will be eliminated. We will cease comparing ourselves with others, seeking to determine who is most important.

Many of us have had the painful experience of striking our thumb with a hammer. When a concerned observer hears our shriek and asks what the problem is, we reply, "I hurt my thumb." But actually the thumb is only the locality where "I" hurt. In terms of our analogy, Paul observes, "If one member suffers, all suffer together; if one member is honored, all rejoice together" (vs. 26). Every member of Christ's body who feels unimportant or useless is a problem for the rest of the body.

At one time I thought this chapter taught that despite great diversity among Christians in any congregation there is still unity. The point, rather, is that precisely *in* this diversity is God's plan for unity, not *in spite* of the diversity (Rom. 12:4-6).

Just as God has made people different in so many ways, God intends that we in the body of Christ be diverse. Attempts to insist on a uniformity of abilities, roles and ministries is a tendency toward the "all eye" view of the church as the body of Christ, which is not a body at all. The church functions best and ministers best to others when this divine intent is recognized and encouraged among the members.

Desiring Unifying Gifts (12:27-31)

A common expression to describe someone who becomes so interested in details that he is unable to see how they relate to the whole is: he is unable to see the forest for the trees. Both in ancient Corinth and in modern America that is a common problem. Because of our stress on the individual we are more likely to see just the "trees."

In 12:27 when Paul begins to conclude this discussion of the diversity of Christ's body, he mentions the body as primary. "You are the body of Christ, and individually members of it." We tend to think of the church as the sum total of its members. But 1 Corinthians 12 reverses the priorities. The body (of Christ) is first, then there are members. The church is much more than the sum total of its members. It is only because there is Christ, whose body we are, that there are individual Christians as members.

One of the best examples of the relationship between the members and the whole is the story of Achan in Joshua chapter 7. The story is familiar—an Israelite commander disobeyed God's instructions about the spoils of war and took some valuables for himself. But Achan's sin caused grief not only for himself. In fact, the wrong first became known because Israel experienced an unexpected and serious defeat in battle.

In our individualistic reading of events, God should have said, "Achan has sinned!" rather than "Israel has sinned" (Joshua 7:11). But the strong relationship between the individual and the whole nation made the sin of one member the concern of the whole.

God has appointed various roles and gifts for Christians in the body of Christ, and these are not all the same (vss. 27-30). Even such a highly valuable gift as *apostle* was limited to a dozen. Men did not choose these gifts, nor should they seek to possess them all. God distributes them as he wills.

The Greek clearly indicates that all the rhetorical questions of verses 29 and 30 assume a negative answer. So we might paraphrase, "All are not apostles, are they?" etc. Thereby the various gifts are shown to be a unifying factor precisely in their diversity. On this basis we are urged to "earnestly desire" the higher gifts (12:31). These gifts unite when guided by love (1 Cor. 13) and when exercised to benefit the whole church (1 Cor. 14).

The Corinthians were led to mutual jealousy and recriminations in considering their gifts because their individualism led them to look at each individual rather than the body. They missed the dimension of the body as the place to belong to the Lord and each other. They regarded the Spirit as a means of private achievement and a source of individual pride. In summary, they had the wrong understanding of gifts, the Spirit, and the church! The common denominator to this failure was their individualism. James Moffatt has well summarized the main point of the chapter about mutual involvement through the Spirit:

> The Spirit is not identified with what the devout soul does with his loneliness, much less with religious self-expression, but with what each is and does for the fellowship.

[1] James Moffatt, *The First Epistle of Paul to the Corinthians* (New York: Harper and Row, 1938), p. 184. Used by permission.

Love Builds Belonging

11

1 Corinthians 13:1-13

The old slogan is, "familiarity breeds contempt." Perhaps that is too strong to apply to reading Scripture, but it does seem that our familiarity with the Bible makes it difficult at times to really hear what it has to say.

Our common practice of memorizing 1 Corinthians 13 as a poem may lead us to mistakenly regard it as independent from its place in 1 Corinthians. However, this chapter about love is bracketed by two chapters which discuss the nature and use of spiritual gifts. This means 1 Corinthians 13 teaches how Christians are to employ their religious abilities and gifts. Although the chapter may be usefully applied to labor negotiations, domestic life, and even international politics, its main purpose is to instruct us in living together in Christ Jesus.

Another mistake arises when we concentrate on 1 Corinthians 13 alone. We fail to notice that 1 Corinthians 13 actually begins with 12:31. Paul concludes chapter 12 on spiritual gifts in the church by saying, "earnestly desire the higher gifts." He then continues, "and I will show you a still more excellent way" (NEB translation: "I will show you the best way of all").

At one time I thought that in chapter 13 Paul set forth

faith, hope and especially love as the highest of the gifts—above tongues, prophecy, miracles, etc. However, after more study, I have now come to believe that Paul here contrasts love with the gifts. Paul did not deny the reality or value of the gifts of the Spirit, but he made their value dependent on the love that motivated them.

Finally, one other mistaken way of studying 1 Corinthians is to focus on 13:10, "when that which is perfect is come," and its relation to 13:8 which foretells the demise of tongues. Literally dozens of articles have been written in popular and scholarly journals with virtually every conceivable interpretation. This, it seems to me, is to focus upon the palpitations and not the pulse. The main point of the chapter is how Christians are to live with each other in the present, how all Christian worship and service, including spiritual gifts, ought to be employed in love. Love builds the sense of belonging in the church.

Love Supersedes (13:1-3)

There is a scene in Ibsen's classic play, *Peer Gynt*, where the hero watches secretly as another young man cuts off his finger so he will not be drafted for military service. Peer Gynt thinks to himself that he can understand the plan, even the desire to take such extreme action. But the will to do it! That is altogether another matter.

This may be the case with Christian love. It is not really too hard to locate the center of the gospel. The familiar John 3:16: "God so loved the world that he gave his only son" simply puts into very concise form the message found throughout the New Testament (see Rom. 5:8; 8:32-39; Eph. 2:4-7; 1 John 4:9, 10). Nor is it too hard to show the demand for Christians to have this same love towards each other (Matt. 22:37-40; Rom. 13:8-10;

Gal. 5:14). There is no reason to believe the Corinthians were less aware of these teachings on love than Paul's other churches—or less aware than we are.

However, it is a very big step from admitting the demand to love in theory and actualizing it in practice. In almost every quarrel between Christians, one will hear the statement, "I know we are supposed to love, *but* . . ." Paul begins his evaluation of love in 1 Corinthians 13 by tactfully putting his observations in the first person ("I"). As he evaluates spiritual gifts, in each and every case he considers the relationship to love.

Paul takes first the gift most prized by the Corinthians. If one were able to speak with great eloquence or even as angels (some scholars feel the Corinthians may have regarded their "tongues" as an angelic speech), unless love is there, the sounds are only clanging and clashings. (Gongs and cymbals were often used in pagan worship to excite the worshippers.) The point is that the greatest enthusiasm and religious excitement count for nothing without love.

Secondly, Paul mentions prophesying, the gift he himself prizes most (14:1, 5). He concludes it also is worthless without love. Indeed, the same can be said for all other spiritual gifts, including wonder-performing faith and even the ultimate self-sacrifice. (A few years before this a visiting guru from India had immolated himself at the international games in Corinth and thereby became a famous person.)

Today many Christians have wondered if they would have the courage to endure persecution for being a Christian as some earlier generations have done. It is clear from 1 Corinthians 13:1-4 that this is not the most important question. Rather than ask if we would *die willingly* for the faith, we need to ask whether we will *live lovingly* for it!

Paul is not just comparing his preference in gifts to that of the Corinthians here. He is saying both the gift you favor, and that I favor, and all others, are equally valueless without love. The spiritually gifted Christian without love remains a pagan.

Love Acts (13:4-7)

What does the Bible mean by love? Probably most Christians today have heard a sermon which contrasted the various Greek words for love (*eros, philia, storgē,* and *agapē*). In fact, *agapē* has almost become an English word by its frequent use among Christians. However, we, like the Corinthians, have some difficulty in relating what we know about love to problems we confront daily.

In 1 Corinthians 13:4-7 Paul not only asserts the primacy of love but describes in some detail how love functions. Love is defined in a *functional* way: what it does and does not do. (A more detailed and very helpful treatment of verses 4-7 is found in Tony Ash's book, *Decide to Love*, Sweet Publishing Co.)

Patient and kind. Paul begins by stating two characteristics of Christian love—patience and kindness. Patience must be very important, for it recurs (although using a different Greek word) in verse 7 where we read: "Love . . . endures all things." It must have taken a great deal of patience for Paul himself as he dealt with the Corinthians. That church was plagued with moral failures and internal divisions, yet prided itself on its wisdom and maturity! Many of us in Paul's situation would be tempted to throw up our hands and say, "I give up! You people are hopeless!" But love demands great patience with people as they grow—and fail—as Christians.

If anything was in short supply in Corinth it was kindness. Whether it was dragging each other before the courts (6:1-8), or insisting on personal rights even when others were harmed (6:8), or the abuse of the poor at the Lord's Table (11:17-33), the Corinthians failed to treat each other kindly.

Normally we associate kindness with fairly minor events, but the New Testament speaks of God's *kindness* which leads to salvation (1 Peter 2:3 and Titus 3:4). Perhaps it is more concrete to speak of kindness than love. We understand kindness, in part because we are so irritated when others are unkind to us.

Neither jealous or boastful. Turning to a negative approach, Paul begins to describe what love is not. First, he says, it is neither jealous or boastful.

These two characteristics are very appropriate for the particular problem of spiritual gifts in the chapters surrounding 1 Corinthians 13. Increased jealousy and boasting about spiritual gifts occurred among the various members. This mutual criticism is addressed in the description of the body of Christ in 1 Corinthians 12. Some believers were jealous of those with more "flashy" gifts, and apparently those who had these gifts boasted of their superiority.

We may think that jealousy and boasting are opposite attitudes, but in reality they have a common basis—a feeling of insecurity. It is easy to understand that jealousy comes from insecurity. If we fear we are unacceptable to others or to God, we covet those qualities in others which we think make them worthy. Most often those who boast of their accomplishments are really afraid they are not capable or successful enough. This is true in business with the "super salesman"; it is true in social life with status climbers or name droppers, and it is even true among Christians who boast to assure themselves they are of value to God.

Christians who are boastful of their abilities and gifts

as well as those who are jealous of others have forgotten that it is God who has so endowed them (1:5-7). We have no reason to boast of what was simply a gift from another and does not reflect any achievement of our own (4:7).

Neither arrogant or rude. The word translated "arrogant" is literally "puffed up" and recalls 8:1: "Knowledge puffs up," Paul's criticism of the Corinthians who were proud of their wisdom. The word also occurs in 4:6 and 19 regarding the Corinthians' improper response to the incest among their members. Clearly "over inflation" of the ego is a Corinthian characteristic. But it is the reverse of love.

"Rudeness" seems rather trivial in comparison with the other attitudes discussed in these verses. However, both in Corinth and today, do not many destructive conflicts among Christians arise not from some blatant or serious moral offense, but simply from hurt feelings resulting from inconsiderateness or rudeness to one another?

An initial infection is quite often something minor (like a cold), but a serious physical illness (such as pneumonia) may result. This is also often true when Christians fight among themselves. When we have been slighted or embarrassed or had our feelings hurt, then we are more prone to attack others or doubt the genuineness of their commitment. While eliminating rudeness will not solve our problems, it may produce an atmosphere in which problems can be faced.

Does not insist on its own way. That Christians consider the needs of the other person has been the admonition in all of 1 Corinthians. Certainly this aspect of love is much needed in Corinth, for their internal divisiveness resulted from its absence.

Again, this problem can be easily seen in worship assemblies. Some Corinthians were determined to exercise their spiritual gifts *as* they wished, *when* they wished. That is why Paul writes that God is not the source of confusion—but of peace (14:33).

As Christians we have a powerful motive for not insisting that our own preferences be followed. The implication of the cross is that Christ did not insist on his own rights but sought the benefit to others (2 Cor. 8:9). He also asks this of his followers (Luke 9:23; Rom. 6:3-11).

Not irritable or resentful. Of all the demands of love, I find most challenging the call not to be irritable. A long wait at a store's check-out counter, or the repeated arguing with my sons after I have said "no," or continuing difficulties with other Christians—in these and other ways, I find it hard to avoid irritation.

Irritability is really a form of pride. It assumes, "Why should such an important person as I be inconvenienced or bothered by you?" Also we often feel that those who irritate us act from insincere motives. ("You're just doing that to irritate me.") I suspect that some Corinthians felt that those Christians who claimed that sacrificial meat was a serious problem for them were only making an issue with insincere motives.

Resentment usually results from our feeling neglected or having personal importance overlooked. We often resent others intruding on our time, causing us to give up our plans for what we feel are lesser matters.

This also relates to internal church conflicts. A person or group of people feels slighted by the elders, preacher, or a teacher. Yet often those they blame are unaware of doing any injury. This lack of awareness is perceived as an intentional neglect and leads to resentment. When we are resentful for wrongs we have endured, whether real or imagined, we are also very quick to take offense at any other slight. In large measure we become the source of our own anguish.

Never rejoices at the wrong, but rejoices in the right. Perhaps you have heard the quip about some hypochondriac, "He has enjoyed ill health for years!" Although an apparent contradiction, some people truly do find fulfillment in their illnesses because this gives them the attention from others which they greatly desire. Similarly, it is a contradiction that anyone, especially a Christian, would rejoice in the wrong.

Possibly Paul has in mind here some in Corinth who actually took pride in doing wrong. 1 Corinthians 5:2 has been so interpreted. Or perhaps he means although the church was seriously endangered by sin, the Corinthians failed to see this threat and continued in their pride as if they were perfect (6:1-8 and especially chap. 8). Yet a more dangerous possibility exists.

I suspect that some in Corinth were finding pleasure in the sins of other Christians so that they could point the accusing finger. This is not really hard to imagine, strange as it may seem at first. If some brother is negligent in attendance, and we later learn that his marriage is also endangered, there is a temptation to say, "I knew this would happen." If someone is converted from a very corrupt past and subsequently relapses into sin, are we filled with sorrow, or do we smugly think, "Well, what can you expect of such folks?"

Love does not rejoice at the failures of others because it seeks their best interests. Jesus wept over Jerusalem, not because of what it would do to him, but because of what Jerusalem did to itself in rejecting him (Matt. 23:37). The body image in 1 Corinthians 12 makes the point about suffering with others—each member is affected with the anguish of any member.

Love never quits. Those who have suffered torture in

prisoner of war camps have often testified that they were sustained by their belief that they would ultimately be freed. It is when we are unable to see an end to the road that we are tempted to give up. If I had to pick the most *difficult* aspect of what 1 Corinthians 13 teaches about love, it would be the message of verse 7—love never quits.

When Christians are differing with each other, what they need most of all is to persevere in working out the problems. I suspect that the strong Christians who disregarded those who would not eat the idol meat gradually grew tired of hearing their objections and said, "That's it. I'm through fooling with them."

Whenever we feel we have been under-appreciated, over-taxed, misunderstood and abused, it is very easy to "write off" other people. We must continually be reminded that "love never gives up."

Love Lasts (13:8-13)

In 1 Corinthians 13:8-13 love is contrasted with the spiritual gifts on the basis of durability. Whether and when gifts have ceased are secondary considerations in the argument of the chapter. What Paul stresses and what the Corinthians (and we) need is that which abides—love.

The qualitative superiority of love is stated in two ways. First, love is *complete*, gifts are *partial*. Various spiritual gifts were given different members, according to God's plan (12:4-11). But love is for all believers, because it is the character of God (1 John 4:8).

Second, love is superior because it is eternal. Although love, the very nature of God, is part of the eternal things, in Christ this love is already present for those who belong to him. It is the "presence of eternity."

Translations of verse 13 vary. The KJV says "And now

118

abideth," but what does the "now" mean? (Similar is the RSV.) Does "now" mean at the present time, or "in brief"? Probably both. At the present time faith, hope and love are God's way for Christians, the presence of the eternal among us. Yet it is equally true that all God wants of his people can be summarized in these three realities as well.

Faith, hope, and especially love are decisive for our corporate relationship with other believers. In Corinth this relationship had come apart and become destructive over the issue of spiritual gifts. For any and all relationships among Christians the acid test is love. James Moffatt summarizes it well in saying, "The presence of love as the really essential quality, is the final criterion of Christian fellowship and service. . . ."[1]

[1]Moffatt, *The First Epistle of Paul to the Corinthians*, p. 204

Building Belonging When We Meet

12

1 Corinthians 14:1-40; 16:1-4, 19-20

In 1 Corinthians 14:23 we have a rare glimpse into the actual worship assemblies of an early church. The main issue is the proper role of tongues and prophecy in these assemblies, but it has far-reaching implications for the proper function of Christian gatherings. Because the Corinthians thought of worship as a private transaction between each believer and his Lord, they had no awareness of the role of church assemblies in mutual edification.

It is important to remember the teachings of 1 Corinthians 12 and 13 as we look at 1 Corinthians 14 because those teachings influence directions given in chapter 14. The importance of the body of Christ, as discussed in chapter 12, and the yardstick of love, as discussed in chapter 13, are used to evaluate tongues and public worship.

Emphasis on Edification (14:1-5)

It is probable that the Corinthians' specific question about spiritual gifts is only addressed directly in 1 Corinthians 14. Although tongues and prophecy are contrasted by Paul, both are regarded as the genuine work of the

Spirit. The contrast is not between inspired speech (tongues) and human eloquence (prophecy), but between two forms of speech from God.

Initially Paul contrasts tongues with prophecy in regard to how each influences the assembled worshippers. The one who speaks in tongues speaks only to God, not to other men because no one can understand what he says. Thus only the one speaking may be edified. Since this is Paul's only reference to edifying oneself, it is probably ironic. On the other hand, the one who prophesies does speak to men and thereby strengthens, encourages, and comforts them (14:3). Thus prophecy is superior in edifying the church.

On the basis of their respective value to the whole church, Paul concludes: "He who prophesies is greater than he who speaks in tongues" (14:5). As was true in the matter of eating sacrificial meat (ch. 8) and the practice around the Lord's table (11:17-33), the decisive thing is how other believers are helped.

We learn here about one valuable criterion for evaluating our assemblies. Normally we think of worship as something offered to God and thus consider how we feel he is affected by the worship. However, worship is evaluated here not by the way it affects God but by the way it affects other Christians. It is a reasonable and proper question to ask about our meetings today—how are other Christians affected? Are they edified? Are they strengthened, encouraged, challenged, comforted?

Clarity of Communication (14:6-12)

Of the many occupations which I would not care to pursue, perhaps heading the list would be junior high band director. Although I did not realize it when I was in a school band, I know now that one has to listen to a lot of noise while waiting for very little music!

The difference between playing an instrument and making music is the first of three illustrations which Paul employs in 14:6-12 to show how prophecy has greater value than tongues. Unless an instrument plays intelligible and distinct notes, it makes noise, not music. If the bugler gives unclear notes the battle may very well be lost. In the third illustration Paul reflects that there are "doubtless many different languages in the world, and none is without meaning" (14:10). However, if we do not know the meaning of a language, it separates us from the speaker and makes us "foreigners."

The truth which these analogies illustrate is in verse 12. If you are zealous for spiritual gifts, seek those which build up the entire church. Similar admonitions are made in 9:19-23; 10:31-33; and 12:7. Apart from the issue of tongues, can we use this criterion as we consider our assemblies today?

Surely these verses imply that our worship also ought to be intelligible and thus serve to build up the entire church. Using English, or any other regional language, does not insure clear communication. Some language is obscure and antiquated. The words of some hymns are difficult to understand. For example, do we know what we're saying when we sing, "here I raise my Ebenezer"? Other language may be too contemporary and is really jargon. The first test of prayers, sermons, hymns, and even reading Scripture is not whether it is catchy and memorable but whether it is plain and understandable.

Criteria for Assemblies (14:13-19)

No doubt there are a number of ways to have acceptable worship which incorporates prayer, song, and message. However, are there any criteria to be used in evaluating worship? In 14:13-19 we have three guidelines, two of which have appeared earlier in some form.

The first guideline is that the mind should be active. The Greek concept of "ecstacy" was that a man became so intimately involved with the deity that he "stood outside" his mind. Perhaps Paul is addressing this problem here. He tells us that we must use reason as well as feelings in worship. Few would contest that a "warm feeling" in Christian worship is preferable to frigidity, but irrationality is not the way to achieve warmth.

A second guideline, already discussed, is whether the congregation is built up (14:17). The concern to edify others, not one's self, is a recurring motif in the letter, probably because Corinthian individualism tended to ignore the needs of others altogether. The same difficulty exists today when we plan our worship thinking only about what "edifies me." The meeting of different and legitimate needs of worshippers may be one of the best reasons for varying our songs, sermons, and order of worship at times.

The third guideline is that all members be able to participate (14:16). Today when one leads prayer, he says "amen," and to hear a repeated "amen" from others is something of a shock. But in earlier days, Christians voiced together their approval of prayers and sermons with interspersed "amens." The Latin scholar Jerome reported the amen resounded in the Roman basilicas of his day like a clap of thunder! While it is perhaps a small thing, responding with an "amen" could be one means to allow members to realize their participation.

The contrast in 1 Corinthians 14 is not between "speaking with the mind/understanding" or "speaking with the Spirit." The contrast is between "speaking with the mind" and speaking without the mind engaged. Our minds and the Spirit are compatible in worship.

The strong contrast between speaking with understanding and without it becomes clear in 14:19. Paul claims that he, like the Corinthians, has the gift of tongues—indeed more so! But as he evaluates worship, Paul finds five intelligible words preferable to 10,000 words in tongues.

Concern for Outsiders (14:20-25)

There has always been some confusion, in my experience, about the expected influence Christian worship should have on outsiders. In general we have sought to have services which visitors would view favorably and find pleasant. This concern for how our worship affects non-Christians is legitimate.

Thus far in chapter 14 Paul has considered only how tongues and prophecy affect members. Now he reflects on how outsiders may respond if they attend a Christian service of worship. Here too tongues are a potential detriment, for upon hearing a number of unintelligible speakers in disorder the visitor will be led to conclude, "You are mad!" (14:23). In Acts 2:13 witnessing tongues even lead some to suspect drunkenness.

Prophecy, on the other hand, has a beneficial effect on outsiders. They are led to self-examination, confession, worship of God and even conversion (14:24, 25). Note that the outsider is not said to be impressed with the Christians or their talents in worship. Rather, the outsider evaluates *his own* life. The decisive thing is not "You really are enthusiastic," but "God is really among you." Worship is most meaningful to outsiders when it points beyond the worshipers to the one who is worthy of worship.

Call for Order (14:26-40)

My childhood memories of worship planning are of a half-dozen men at the front of the auditorium, between Sunday School and the morning worship assembly, deciding who would do what. From that rather casual manner many churches have moved to a worship planning committee. Often plans are made and a printed program of worship is prepared.

The worship order in Corinth, which we see implicitly in this epistle, seems to resemble my childhood experiences more than the present trends. It was a rather loose, spontaneous worship in which "*each one* (to be taken literally, with a majority of the members leading in some way) has a hymn, a word of instruction, a revelation," etc. Of course the Corinthian congregations were small and met in the close confines of first-century houses. The danger in the public worship in Corinth was not dullness, but disorder.

Paul seemingly does not seek to stop what they are doing but tries to give order to it. He seeks to insure that "all things must be done for the building up of the church" (14:26). In seeking to secure this order, he gives some directions which were as revolutionary in his day as they are commonplace today.

First, Paul says if tongues are employed they are to be of a limited number (14:27) and are not to be included without an interpreter. Without an interpreter those who wish to use tongues are to do so in their own homes and not "in church." (Verse 28 has a rather unusual use of the word "church" to mean the assembly, rather than the body of people.) If those who wish to speak in tongues do have an interpretation provided, then tongues become prophecy—since what distinguishes the one from the other is that everyone can understand prophecy (14:5)!

Second, rather matter-of-factly, Paul says that even if one receives a revelation he must wait for another who is speaking to finish. "For the spirits of the prophets are subject to the control of the prophets" (14:32). In the Greek tradition one of the marks of receiving a divine message (as with the Delphic oracle) was that the recipient lost control of him/herself. It is a real modification of this view—surely known by the Corinthians—when Paul demands that everyone take care to wait his turn to speak.

Some have concluded from the description of the Corinthian worship that modern worship should follow this example of spontaneity, with each one contributing as he wishes. Even some who consider this idea impractical in large congregations wistfully long for such a practice as more "spiritual."

However, in view of the entire letter it seems more accurate to say that Paul is seeking to produce order at Corinth, not make their spontaneous practice serve as a guide for later generations. He seeks to make a very unpredictable worship far more predictable.

It would be just as wrong, on the other hand, to conclude that Paul teaches we should follow a prescribed form, where anyone can predict what will come next. He does leave room in this chapter for individuals to actively participate in turn and in order.

Burton Coffman has a balanced observation on the relationship between structure and informality in worship:

> The spontaneous, informal nature of the early church services is clearly visible . . . There cannot be any doubt that formalism, which is the current religious style, and which certainly corrected the shameful disorders like those at Corinth, has nevertheless, left many a congregation in a state of abiosis."[1]

Almost as an afterthought, Paul concludes this discussion of spiritual gifts by mentioning the role of women in worship. To avoid reading too much into this passage, we need to consider the passage's original intent. Since these verses conclude a discussion about tongue-speaking, it seems reasonable to conjecture that was the topic addressed in 14:34-35. If so, the point would be that women are not to employ the gift of tongue-speaking in the assembly at all, even in the presence of the required interpreter (14:27, 28). To understand verses 33-35 as forbidding all speaking by women in church assemblies causes a conflict between Paul's instructions of 11:2-16 and 14:34-36, with women permitted to speak in one place and forbidden in the other.

Acts of Caring (16:1-4, 19, 20)

As in other letters, Paul's final chapter deals with several miscellaneous issues, including personal greetings. Two items mentioned especially relate to what should happen when Christians come together.

The collection (16:1-4). The collection which Paul undertook to raise among the Gentile churches for the poor in Jerusalem is like a subterranean stream. It surfaces briefly in Paul's letters in unexpected places, but is really very important.

The contribution was begun to meet a practical need in Judea (Acts 11:28-30; Gal. 2:10). Paul saw in it something greater, a means for Gentile Christians to share with Jewish Christians and thus manifest the unity of the gospel (Rom. 15:27). The collection then was not simply a practical necessity, but a "grace" (2 Cor. 8:4), a "fellowship" (*koinonia*, 2 Cor. 8:4; Rom. 15:26), a ministry (Rom. 15:31; 2 Cor. 9:1, 2).

Today our contribution is not for the Jerusalem poor, nor do we anticipate Paul's arrival to take it. But just as Paul used this project as a concrete means of showing the reconciliation found in Christ and the unity of Christian fellowship, so today it is right to point beyond the practical uses to the religious meaning of giving.

Occasionally the collection is viewed as a financial intrusion into the more "spiritual" prayers, songs, and communion. This is mistaken. Giving is described as a "fellowship" (*koinonia*, 2 Cor. 8:4, the same word used to describe the Lord's Supper in 1 Cor. 10:16, 17). How can we make concrete our awareness of the implications of Christ's sacrifice? One means is the contribution, which is caring for the body for which Christ died.

The kiss of peace (16:19, 20). Like the contribution, the "kiss of peace" or "holy kiss" is mentioned often in the New Testament but never dwelt on (Rom. 16:16; 2 Cor. 13:12; 1 Thess. 5:26; 1 Peter 5:14). This common greeting was, and is today, widely found in the Mediterranean world. Among Christians it marked their status as "brethren" in Christ.

Many have noted that this custom was culturally based and then concluded it isn't necessary in our different culture. Obviously it is cultural, but that is not sufficient. When they came together the kiss of peace was their means of expressing the caring relationship in Christ. Certainly we are as much or more in need of such expression of mutual caring in our assemblies as they were. It seems worthwhile to practice an expression appropriate to our culture when the church assembles.

Recovering Worship

Like the Corinthians, we today wrongly tend to evaluate worship on private and personal criteria. How am I affected? Do I like it? Do I feel better afterwards? The question to begin with should be, "How is the whole community of faith affected?" The criterion for Christians is whether edification of the corporate life occurs (14:5, 12, 17). The criterion for non-Christians is whether those who attend consider God. Did their encounter with Christian worship lead them to look beyond the assembled worshipers to the God who is worshipped (14:23-25)? If these criteria are met, worship assemblies make the church a place to belong.

[1]Burton Coffman, *A Commentary on 1 and 2 Corinthians* (Austin, Texas: Firm Foundation Publishing House, 1977), p. 236. Used by permission.

Belonging Forever

13

1 Corinthians 15:1-58

The fifteenth chapter of 1 Corinthians cuts to the vital center of Christian faith—the resurrection. Like previous chapters it addresses concrete problems of individualism within the congregation. Some of the Corinthians had lost the significance of the resurrection by regarding it as a topic of debate and speculation. Today we also may fail to appreciate the central importance of the resurrection. Therefore, Paul's message to the Corinthians is equally valuable for us.

The problem the Corinthians were having was not denying the resurrection of Jesus but that Christians would be raised (15:12). They were probably influenced by a combination of their strong individualism as Greeks and their (mis)interpretation of Paul's preaching.

A Cultural Problem

Currently much interest has been stirred in the experiences of persons who have recovered from "near death" encounters. Perhaps all societies have speculated on such events because death is a universal phenomenon, and mankind has difficulty believing death is our final destination.

Corinth was no different. As a Greek city, it presumably was influenced by some of the Greek philosophers' and poets' beliefs about death. In general, Hellenistic thought had very little hope for any life beyond the grave. Only a few exceptional individuals ("heroes"), such as Hector and Achilles, became eternal. The great mass of humanity could only expect extinction. This could be regarded either as a great, unavoidable tragedy, or, like life, simply a natural process.

When Greek thinkers did contemplate a life after death, it was based on the "immortality of the soul." The "soul" or "mind" was regarded as a divine spark within each man which returned to the "world Soul" (or God) upon his death. This version of life after death robs people of their individual existence because their souls are dissolved into the one eternal being.[1]

Unlike Greeks, most Jews did believe in life beyond death and in a resurrected body, not survival of the soul. Some Old Testament passages, such as Psalm 73:24, Job 19:25-27, Isaiah 26:19, and Daniel 12:1-2, anticipate life after death. By the time of Jesus most of the Jews, especially the Pharisees, firmly held the hope for resurrection.

When early Christians preached of a coming resurrection of people's bodies, most Jews easily accepted this. However, because of their different cultural background, the Corinthians rejected this promised resurrection of their bodies.

The Secure Foundation (15:1-11)

Although the issue raised at Corinth was the resurrection of believers, Paul begins with the resurrection of Jesus as the secure foundation for confidence in our own resurrection. In the first eleven verses of chapter 15 he recalls the common ground he shares with the Corinthians about resurrection.

Paul restates in 1 Corinthians 15:3-8 the most basic message Christian evangelists preach. According to Scripture, this basic formulation of the gospel is the death, burial, and resurrection of Jesus, and the subsequent appearing to his disciples. This basic outline was handed on within the church's mission (15:3) and was shared by all the earliest witnesses (15:11) as well as by those who heard them (15:1, 2). The sermons in Acts elaborate this formulation of the gospel's core.

The resurrection is really the pulse of the New Testament. On this basis Jesus authorized evangelism (Matt. 28:16-20; John 11:25), the confession of faith in him (Rom. 10:9), and the decisive part of mission (Acts 26:22-23). Even with the Corinthian congregation's difficulties about resurrection of believers, Paul was confident they believed in Jesus' raising. It is on the basis of a common belief about Jesus that Paul begins his argument about the future for those in Christ.

Are Dead Persons Raised? (15:12-34)

Several years ago a popular song recounted the stages of life and its futility and wistfully asked, "Is that all there is?" If so, the lyric advises, let's lose ourselves in drink and merriment.

There are two points in the song which bear on 1 Corinthians 15. First, Paul points out life has a doubtful meaning if this is all there is. Second, what we believe about death affects how we live life. Paul quotes Isaiah 22:13 (although parallel sentiments abound in Greek writings) to the effect, "If 'this life' is *the* life, then the sensible way of living is to enjoy it to the full." [2]

If not Christians, then not Christ (vss. 12-19). First Corinthians 15:12 recounts the Corinthians' argument. Some said, "There is no resurrection of the dead." Their basis for arguing against the resurrection is not clear.

Possibly they held the materialists' viewpoint. Materialists reject the resurrection because they say there is no other part of life but the physical. Mankind is in the same situation as the little ditty says of the dog: "I had a dog; his name was Rover. When he lived, he lived in clover. When he died, he died all over."

A second possibility is that their objection to resurrection came from the Greek view of mankind. Greek philosophy says the body itself is *incapable* of spiritual service. It is like a husk to be discarded when death releases the inner spirit. This view is capsulized in a Greek pun—*some-sema*, which means "the body is a tomb" (from which we need release). This may have been the Corinthian view, for in 15:35-57 Paul addresses the problem of the nature of the resurrection body.

The third and most probable interpretation of the Corinthian disbelief is that they felt they had already entered into complete spiritual life as proven by their spiritual gifts, especially tongues. Second Timothy 2:18 proves that some Christians held this view. The Corinthians were so satisfied in their present possession of the Spirit that they awaited no greater blessing.

In reply to their denial Paul points to the basic confession which all Christians share about Jesus (15:1-11). He concludes if, as some Corinthians argue, "Dead people do not rise," then Christ, whom they confessed *died* for our sins, has not risen either (15:13). This implies, in turn, that the apostolic preaching is "vain" (better "empty"), for that is what they preach about Jesus.

Tragic consequences of denying the resurrection continue to pile up. Paul restates the connection between Christ's resurrection and that of believers (15:16). If indeed there is no resurrection of the dead, then the faith which the Corinthians confess (5:2) is empty, and they remain in their sins (15:17). Further, those Christians who have already died are simply lost (15:18), for they believed a false message preached by liars. Did they belong to God and his people only in this life?

The negative conclusions are summed up in 15:19. If our faith in Christ relates only to this life, we are a pitiable lot. Men should shake their heads at these lamentable folks who have changed their lives based on a mistaken trust in Jesus.

But, thank God, this is not so! (vss. 20-28). In contrast to the sense of apprehension and doubt in verses 12-19, a shift is signaled with "But now." It is as a breath of fresh air when in verses 20-28 Paul positively states the case for our resurrection. He sketches the events between the present time and the consummation, explaining how the resurrection of Christ necessarily leads to the resurrection of Christians.

Christ's resurrection, Paul says, was the "first fruits" of a coming harvest. In agriculture the "first fruits" are considered a sign of a promised harvest. This metaphor clarifies the resurrection of Christians in two ways. Christ's resurrection is a proof of our own resurrection. And Christ's resurrection, as the first fruits, makes clear that our resurrection is still awaited (Rom. 8:23; Col. 1:13; and 2 Cor. 1:22).

By his resurrection from the dead, Christ has representatively broken death's hold which has ruled all men since Adam (15:21, 22; Rom. 5:12-18). In this way Christ is the vanguard of our resurrection. He resembles Adam because, like Adam, he potentially affects all humanity.

The teaching about the resurrection in these verses walks a tightrope. While seeking to establish firmly the certainty of our resurrection, Paul must, at the same time, teach that our resurrection is still to be awaited. "Now" Christ (not Christians) is risen from the dead. The order is: *now* Christ; *then*, at his coming, (and not before!) those who belong to him. Then comes the End. Now is the time of the preaching of the gospel, the life of the church, and—waiting. Those Corinthians who believed they had already reached their spiritual zenith needed to hear this. There is still a period of conflict existing between Christ's resurrection and the time when the "last enemy" (15:26) is defeated and victory is complete (15:28).

Other absurdities (vss. 29-34). Leaving positive arguments about the future resurrection, Paul considers more implications of its denial and thus its necessity. Three arguments are given here: first, denying the resurrection makes baptism meaningless (15:29); second, it makes suffering for the gospel senseless (15:30-32), and third, it leads to an irreligious life style (15:33-34).

"Baptism of the dead" is a well-known chestnut of biblical interpretation. Over thirty solutions have been suggested.[3] Here we must settle for two observations. First, the argument assumes the Corinthians know and practice "baptism for the dead," and thus Paul argues *from* their practice, not *for* it. Second, this baptism—like all baptism—is meaningless if Christ is not raised, because in baptism Christians believe they appropriate Christ's death *and resurrection* for themselves (Rom. 6:3-11).

A second argument from absurdity is that if there is no resurrection, why should apostles, and others, risk their lives preaching this gospel of the resurrection? Their activity is foolish in two ways. First, they are preaching a lie (15:14, 15), and second, they are paying dearly for their preaching (15:31, 32).

The third argument is that denial of resurrection leads to a corrupt life style. A close relationship exists between doctrine and morals. Although some humanists live very upright lives without a belief in God and some professed Christians blaspheme their profession by their

135

lives, in the broad picture it still seems that faith in God
provides a basis for secure morality that is absent without such faith. In this way Paul correctly argues that believing "Let us eat and drink, for tomorrow we die" will
lead to "Bad company ruins good morals" (15:32, 33).

How Are the Dead Raised? (15:35-50)

There is a fascinating little book by E. A. Abbott en-
titled, *Flatland: A Romance of Many Dimensions*. It is a
science-fiction work dealing with principles of higher
physics. In it a citizen of a two-dimensional world called
"Flatland," who has known only length and width, encounters a visitor from the world of three dimensions.
This visitor seeks to explain the third dimension, thick-
ness or depth. But how do you explain a third dimension
to one who knows only two? After a personal visit to
Spaceland, the Flatlander returns a believer and tries to
convince his fellow Flatlanders of this "other dimension." They are unconvinced and have him put away to be
cured of odd ideas.

The Bible, and 1 Corinthians 15 in particular, has a
similar difficulty in speaking of the resurrection to those
who have no experience with this "dimension" of human
life. Without experience one lacks both the personal understanding and an adequate vocabulary to describe the
reality. Thus the nature of the resurrection body is discussed here largely with analogies.

The Corinthians' second question about the resurrection which Paul quotes in 15:35 is, "Some one will ask,
'How are the dead raised? With what body do they
come?'" Although these may be genuine questions, they
probably were really objections to resurrection, implying
"A resurrection body is inconceivable." At least Paul answers as if the questions were insincere: "Fool!"

Paul addresses the questions with a series of analogies. The first (15:36-38) is of grain and harvest. This

analogy answers the first question "*How* are the dead raised?" (Compare Jesus in John 12:24.) The analogy shows the relationship between death and new life, the difference between what is sown and what is harvested.

The second analogy notes that creation shows God's ability to provide a body for everything as needed for its role in the universe, whether heavenly or terrestrial. This analogy shows that Paul does not even consider the possibility of a "naked" soul, without a body. Even in 2 Corinthians 5:1-5 the hope is not to be "unclothed," but to be further clothed.

In 15:35-41, Paul continues a series of contrasts of the present body and the resurrection body. Having established the certainty of the resurrection body, it is necessary to teach Christians that it is different from this body. This was particularly necessary in Corinth where some may have felt they already had a "resurrection life."

Two things call for explanation in 15:42-50. First, the contrast between the physical, or natural, body and the spiritual body (15:44-48) is not between something "made of spirit stuff" and something made of physical stuff. First Corinthians 10:2, 3 shows that the word "spiritual" (*pneumatikon* in Greek) means "product of a miracle." The contrast is between what man is by virtue of being born and that which he will be at God's miraculous change.

Second, "flesh and blood" in 15:50 means either "natural man" or "living men" in contrast to those who have died. Thus 15:50 tells us that neither those alive nor those who have perished inherit the kingdom of God without the resurrection body which God will give.

The Final Triumph (15:51-58)

Paul concludes his discussion of this most profound and difficult Christian belief by reflecting on the signifi-

cance of resurrection life. He seeks to describe the inde-
scribable, to speak the unspeakable. Thus the chapter
ends with a hymn of praise and victory (15:54, 55).

Two things are noted concerning death. First, death
itself will be swallowed up in divine victory. Those
whom death now holds captive will be released. But this
is in the future, not now. Second, Paul envisions that not
all will die but all will be changed. He does not speculate
on when this will all occur.

This says something important to us. In our times
when things once only whispered secretly are shouted
from every TV or movie, and crude words have become
fashionable, we still recognize one obscenity—death.
Hebrews 2:15 describes a common human experience
when it says that Satan "through the fear of death" holds
men captive all their lives. The release from this bondage
is the resurrection, now available in hope.

This complex discussion comes to a very practical
conclusion (15:58). Because of the Christian hope for
resurrection, we know that work done for Christ has
meaning (1 Thess. 4:15f). The hope of the resurrection
tells us that this bodily life is simply incomplete. The un-
bodily spiritual existence desired by the Corinthians and
their many heirs says this bodily life is meaningless.

The Bible is very realistic in speaking of resurrection
life. For the present it is ours only *in hope*. Only the
Lord has entered it already. For that reason all the sorrows, the effects of past sins, and the difficulties are not
denied. They are real. But the resurrection of Jesus
promises that God will insure our ultimate victory. We
will belong to God and his people forever!

---

[1] Holladay, *The First Letter of Paul to the Corinthians*, pp. 196-97.
[2] Conzelmann, *1 Corinthians*, p. 278.
[3] Holladay, pp. 204-205.

📖Journeys
Adult Bible Studies

Helping Adults Grow

JOURNEYS ADULT BIBLE STUDIES provide
unparalleled resources for your adult Bible study.
These versatile resources effectively guide adults in
exciting studies of God's Word and may be used
by adult Bible classes, special Bible study groups,
ladies' Bible classes, and for personal Bible study.

Nine study options can be the answers to your
group's Bible study needs. Each study is based on
a life-centered paperback and has the unique
JOURNEYS TEACHER'S MANUAL/RESOURCE KIT.

Help these studies come alive for your group with
the **JOURNEYS TEACHER'S MANUAL/RESOURCE KIT.**
KIT includes:

- ■ Teacher's manual which offers 13 practical
  lesson plans for your weekly Bible study

- ■ Two-color overhead transparencies to
  reinforce learning

- ■ 12 Explorer's sheets on duplicator masters

STUDIES NOW AVAILABLE